The CHISEL-TOOTH TRIBE

Wilfrid Swancourt Bronson

The
CHISEL-TOOTH
TRIBE

Written and Illustrated
by

Wilfrid Swancourt Bronson

SUNSTONE
PRESS

SANTA FE

Sunstone books may be purchased for educational, business, or sales promotional use.
For information please write: Special Markets Department, Sunstone Press,
P.O. Box 2321, Santa Fe, New Mexico 87504-2321.

Printed on acid free paper

Library of Congress Cataloging-in-Publication Data

Bronson, Wilfrid S. (Wilfrid Swancourt), 1894-1985.
  The chisel-tooth tribe / written and illustrated by Wilfrid Swancourt Bronson.
    p. cm.
  Originally published: New York : Harcourt, Brace and Co., c1939.
  ISBN 978-0-86534-854-7 (softcover : alk. paper)
  1. Rodents. I. Title.
  QL737.R6B83 2012
  599.35--dc23
                                    2011048696

WWW.SUNSTONEPRESS.COM
SUNSTONE PRESS / POST OFFICE BOX 2321 / SANTA FE, NM 87504-2321 /USA
(505) 988-4418 / ORDERS ONLY (800) 243-5644 / FAX (505) 988-1025

CONTENTS

1

THE CHISEL-TOOTH TRIBE IN GENERAL

ALL over the world except where it is coldest, near the North and South Poles, live animals which belong to the chisel-tooth tribe. Squirrels, woodchucks, beavers, guinea pigs, rabbits, rats and mice, porcupines and so on and on—a thousand different kinds and more. Of each kind there are many thousands of members, of some kinds many millions. It is an enormous tribe of animals though most of the members themselves are not so very large.

But large or small, all members carry a kit of marvelous tools which show that they belong to the tribe and follow the trade of chiseling. The tools they carry are their four front teeth, two upper and two lower, shaped exactly like four chisels, ever razor-sharp. With these they do such an everlasting lot of gnawing that they have the common name of rodents, or animals that gnaw.

When you come to Chapter 2 you will read of many special things about the various members. But this first chapter tells of things about the whole tribe which will make the special things more interesting and easier to understand. For instance, we must explain about the way the chisel-teeth grow, how they are used, and how they are kept from ever growing dull.

A chisel is made of two kinds of metal. The longer side of the blade which cuts or bites into the wood is of very hard steel. The shorter, beveled side is softer iron. The two are welded together to make a very useful tool for carpenters. The tools of the chisel-tooth tribe are made of enamel and ivory which grow together from their jaws. The enamel is the sharp biting edge and the ivory takes the place of the chisel's softer iron. In the drawing you will see that the ivory of the teeth is beveled back from the enamel edge just as the iron is from the steel.

The upper and lower teeth meet in such a way that they grind each other. The ivory wears away the faster, always leaving the hard, thin enamel to form the cutting edge. So a chisel-tooth chap's tools never get dull but with use grow ever sharper. You might suppose that such self-grinding teeth would soon wear out and leave a poor squirrel,

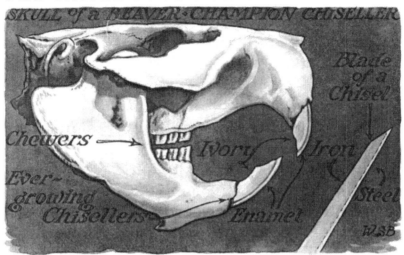

for instance, with no good tools for gnawing through hard nuts, for biting chunks from apples, or for cutting off sweet maple buds to eat. But the chisel-teeth do not grow to a certain size and stop the way ours do. They keep on growing as long as the animal lives, just as your fingernails do, growing just as fast as they are worn away.

But suppose a squirrel, biting something very hard, breaks off one of his chisel-teeth. That is very bad. If he breaks an upper tooth the lower one will have nothing to grind upon. It will grow and grow, curving up and around, and after a while may grow right into the squirrel's eye perhaps. Meanwhile the broken upper tooth keeps on growing; but by the time it is once more as long as it ought to be, the lower tooth is too long and cannot grind it off. So it also grows longer and longer, curving downward and finally sticking into the unlucky little squirrel's throat. If the animal has not starved to death because his teeth won't work well any more, the teeth will finally kill him anyway. This does not happen very often, but when it does it must be awful for the squirrel.

When you hear a tiny mouse making a monstrous racket gnawing in the wall, you may wonder why his teeth aren't broken all to bits. But it takes a lot to break such teeth. Of course the mice gnaw through timbers in our homes to make holes for use as doorways. But I suppose they often gnaw just to keep their teeth ground sharp and short enough. Sometimes they probably gnaw for the fun of it, just as you would enjoy whittling a nice piece of wood if you had a good sharp jackknife handy.

You might expect the mouse gnawing in the wall to get his mouth all full of splinters and perhaps swallow some and choke. This is all very nicely taken care of. None of the chisel-tooth tribe has any canine teeth, no long pointed teeth at the forward corners of their jaws, such as dogs have, or like the eye teeth in our mouths. Between the chisel-teeth and the chewing teeth in their cheeks there is a space where no teeth grow at all. Here the inside skin of their mouths is covered with hair and folds into the space where no teeth grow. So while the front teeth are chiseling away at the wood in the wall, the splinters drop out on either side and never pass the fold of fur between them and the rest of the mouth. Of course, if the mouse is gnawing cheese or other food, the fur is unfolded and the food passes back to be chewed by the cheek teeth and swallowed.

Though their teeth are so unlike our own, the hands and feet of chisel-tooth chaps are quite a lot like ours. I say "hands" because the front feet of all except the hares and rabbits (useful only in digging and swift running) are used as hands as often as they are as feet. As feet they help in running about, but as hands they help at climbing, wash-

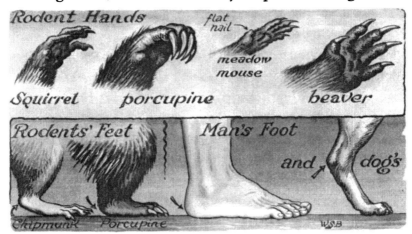

Rodent Hands

flat nail

meadow mouse

Squirrel   porcupine   beaver

Rodents' Feet   Man's Foot   and dog's

Chipmunk   Porcupine

ing, nest-building, and holding food or storing it away for future use. To be sure most of them have hardly any thumb and the fingers have claws instead of nails. But many kinds of chisel-toothers have nails, not claws, on what stubby thumbs they do have. The hind feet have five toes and are used in one way much as we use ours. The human tribe and the chisel-tooth tribe set the entire sole of the foot on the ground. Not like the dog and cat and many other animals which keep their heels up, running only on their toes and the balls of their feet.

The chisel-tooth chaps, or rodents, are so numerous and live in so many different parts of the world that they have many different ways of living. A lot of them, like woodchucks and rabbits, live in burrows of one kind or another, dug in the ground. A few, like the beavers, spend much time in the water and build their houses there. But others, like some of the squirrels, live a great deal in trees and some of these are even able to fly in a gliding sort of way. Most of them are very neat and tidy and very good at making nests and keeping house, which they seem to enjoy. One chisel-tooth chap often has several homes, each provided with a cozy bed and perhaps a good supply of food. Many rodents store up great supplies of food for use in winter, while some just go to sleep and forget about it when cold winds begin to blow. Woodchucks do this, and even some squirrels spend a lot of time in bed while the winter is at its worst.

It is surprising that a creature so very wide awake as the squirrel can go to sleep so soundly. For days and even weeks, through all the coldest spells of winter, he lies curled up in his leaf-lined hole, high in some old tree. Even when the great tree cracks loud and sharp in the night as the dampness in it freezes, he hardly wakes. Perhaps he only dreams of an acorn falling on dry leaves. His woodchuck cousin sleeps still more soundly, never waking up at all till spring. Such long winter sleeping is called hibernation. Many other animals besides rodents hibernate—frogs, garter snakes, and bears, for instance.

At the end of summer when fruits and nuts and seeds are ripe and plentiful, a rodent which must hibernate eats all he can, getting as fat as possible. By the time cold weather comes he has begun to feel quite drowsy. For a time, after frosty nights, when the world warms up for a few hours every day, he may get about and eat some more and doze in the autumn sunshine. But at last steady cold

hibernating

sets in and the fat, logy fellow stays in his bed. All the quickness of the summer has left him. His little heart beats ever more slowly till it scarcely beats at all. Only once in a long while does he take a breath and then it is very slight. If you should hold a mirror under his cold nose there would not be breath enough to make a cloud upon it.

And of course he eats nothing in his long, long sleep. How then does he keep alive? Well, his body is very much like an engine in a way. Cars cannot go unless we feed them gasoline. The gasoline must be mixed with air before it will explode. When it explodes this makes the heat and energy which gives the car its power, its life. The car has cylinders, carburetor, spark plugs, etc. The woodchuck's machinery is his heart and lungs and stomach, etc. It uses a different kind of fuel. But whatever he eats, that is his gasoline. From this and the air he breathes his engine gives him life—the power to run, to dig, to see and hear, to feel and squeal and so on. When the car is standing still with its engine barely running, we say it is idling. It is using very little gas and has almost no power. When the rodent hibernates, his little engine is also idling and he has not even power enough to keep awake.

Since he cannot eat in his sleep, where does his engine get the fuel it needs even though idling? The hibernator has a "fuel tank." It is the thick layer of fat he stored beneath his skin before cold weather came. Slowly and steadily this fat is used to keep his engine going. By spring it has melted quite away. He comes out of bed very thin and hungry. His "fuel tank" and his stomach are empty. He must eat. And so another season of lively wakefulness begins.

Much of the lively wakefulness of rodents comes from their need to watch out constantly for enemies. They have so many. Hawks, eagles, owls, crows, bears, wolves, foxes, dogs, tame cats, wildcats, badgers, minks, weasels, skunks, and other beasts of prey catch every kind of chisel-toother that they can, to eat to keep themselves alive. And men are always hunting them, not only eating rabbits, muskrats, woodchucks, and even porcupines, but killing many others for their fur as well. Perhaps that is why they are such a nervous tribe of animals. The ones that are not nervous get eaten. The nervous ones are ever ready to hide or run away or both. So they live, at least long enough to raise more nervous rodents like themselves.

If you or I were as nervous and had to act as they do, we should become very ill, perhaps die in a short time. Imagine a human family coming downstairs to breakfast, all acting like squirrels. They get halfway downstairs, there is a sound outdoors. What was that? Don't know! Rush back upstairs! This happens several times. Finally all are seated at the table, but not till each one has looked under it and behind the door. Everybody continually stops eating to crane his neck out the window or to look again under the table. Again a sound outdoors. Everyone stops eating and stays in whatever position he happens to be, holding his breath. Nothing happens. Gradually they go on eating again, but always stopping between every two bites to stare in all directions. Suddenly the mailman knocks on the door. Everybody screams, one rushes upstairs, another down cellar, one hangs on the chandelier. How long could you keep it up if you had to live like that? But to a squirrel or other rodent it is perfectly natural. It does not ruin his appetite nor make him miserable.

But though this nervous nature saves the lives of many, every year millions do not escape "the jaws that bite, the claws that catch." It seems as though certain tribes of animals were living in the world just to act as food for other beasts that prey upon them. In the sea there are tribes of fishes which are always eaten in billions by the bigger, fiercer fishes. In the air flying swarms of insects are devoured by birds and bats. And on the land the rodents die to feed other animals which must have meat. That is the way of the animal world, one kind living on another. But the animals which are eaten in great numbers always make up for it by having great numbers of young ones.

On the other hand, if lots of rodents were not killed or eaten, so many young ones would grow up to have more and more young ones of their own that very soon there would not be grass, leaves, fruit, nuts, or grain enough to feed them all and the world would be overrun with starving rodents. Farmers could raise no crops and people would starve. Rats would fill the cities and the world would be a most unpleasant place. So while the rodents are useful as food for beasts of prey, the beasts of prey are useful in keeping the number of rodents from becoming too large. That is what is called the balance of nature.

And what animal is it, do you suppose, which upsets the balance of nature oftenest? It is man. Man often kills his best animal friends, thinking they are enemies. Suppose a farmer who is not well acquainted with wild animals' ways sees an owl or hawk. He shoots it for fear it will catch his chickens. But it may be a kind which only catches rabbits, rats and mice, and woodchucks. The farmer always shoots the hawks and owls not knowing one kind

13

from another. He has already killed off all the foxes, bears, and bobcats which also eat the rabbits, rats and mice, and woodchucks. But rodents increase faster than their enemies which are almost all gone now, except the farmer. He and his barn cat can never kill all the rodents. There are too many of them now. Rabbits and woodchucks eat up his garden, rats take the grain in his barn while field mice spoil his hay and grain fields. He gets a half dozen more cats. But they kill all insect-eating birds about his farm. So then the insects increase and spoil what is left of his garden, fields, and trees. This sort of thing has happened so often that we have had to make laws to keep farmers and the far too many hunters from shooting the wrong creatures and constantly destroying the balance of nature.

It may seem to you a terrible thing to be a rodent born to dodge fierce enemies all one's life, only finally to end up in their stomachs. But it probably does not seem so bad to the rodents. They are easily frightened because they need to be, so that they will dash away from danger before it is too late. But they get quickly over fright. It does not bother them as long as being frightened bothers us. They soon go about their affairs as though nothing had happened to disturb them.

But what about it when they do get caught? Well, I'll make a guess. I guess that a creature suffers more before it is caught than after. I realize that the rabbit which the hounds are chasing is scared, and that the longer it runs the more its tiring body aches. But when a hound finally catches it and gives it a shake, I believe it feels very little pain, if any. I think its feelings become very numb in that last excitement and that most of its fear is gone as well.

After Dr. Livingstone, the great explorer, had been mauled by an African lion, he said that as he fell to the ground under the lion which sank its claws and teeth into

him, he felt no pain or fear although he was not unconscious and saw just what was happening to himself. Only after he was rescued did he suffer from his wounds. Instead of lion let us say pussycat. In place of Dr. Livingstone let us say mouse. Don't you suppose the mouse's feelings would be about the same? I have actually seen a mouse, which a cat was mauling, suddenly bite the cat's tongue when she went to eat it. She howled and spat, and when the mouse let go she sat astonished till it got away. Probably, like Dr. Livingstone after his rescue from the lion, that little mouse felt rather badly once it had escaped. But perhaps not so badly while the cat was catching it.

No wild animal ever has a quiet, peaceful, "happy ending." As soon as their legs grow a little weary and their wits a little slow, they are killed by some enemy who still is strong. Only our pets who share the protection of our homes get a chance to grow old safely.

We cannot blame the strong animals for living on the weak. Everything lives by the dying of other things. We do ourselves. We take eggs from under hens for our breakfasts and cook them with ham or bacon which was once part of a living pig. We have our beef which once was cow, our mutton which was sheep, our chicken and our turkey and so on. Even vegetarians cannot help living by the death of other creatures. The shoes they wear are made of leather taken from the backs of cattle, hogs, and horses. The loaf of bread they eat was once a field of standing grain. In the field lived song sparrows, meadow larks, meadow mice, frogs, garter snakes, and insects. The grain itself was living. When it was cut down a tremendous number of lives were destroyed—just to make a loaf of bread to keep a tender-hearted human being alive. So you see, a hunting animal can never be blamed for killing what it needs to keep itself alive. The only hunter we might blame is the man who

kills wild animals just for fun and not for needed food.

Not everybody realizes that though lions, mice, and people look so little like each other, they all belong to the same great class of creatures known as mammals. It does not matter whether they are people, monkeys, dogs or cats, cows or horses, pigs, sheep, rodents or what not, all are relatives from the very long ago. All mammals are born of mammas who have milk to feed them, all have hair or fur of one kind or another, all have the same kind of warm blood in their veins, and the bones and "innards" of them all are much alike. If mammals were automobiles, we could say that they are of many different models but all have the same type of engine. The bodies of rats and mice and guinea pigs are so similar to ours that doctors study them to find out how to cure some sicknesses that people have.

The doctors also use our chisel-toothed relations in studying the minds of animals. Plenty of people believe that animals cannot think, that they only feel. Of course all animals have feelings, some more, some less. I am sure the chisel-tooth chaps have a great variety of feelings. They can feel bold or timid, gay or unhappy, affectionate or hateful, jealous and stubborn or generous and helpful. And I believe all of them can think some. It seems to me that animals think about the things that matter to them just as we do. The only difference is that more things matter to us and so we have to do more thinking.

There are some very stupid people in the world and

some very bright animals. Between the two I would choose bright animals for company every time. The squirrel who comes to my study door is a more welcome visitor than a dull person would be. For the squirrel has his thinking cap on when he comes to call. He used to curse me from the treetops. He was afraid of me and wanted me to go away. Those were his feelings. But he did some thinking too, I'm sure. And his thoughts overcame his fears.

Because I always left good things to eat about and never made a rush to catch him when he took them, I must not be as terrible as he had supposed. His angry squirrel words no longer could express his idea of me. So he cursed no more. And now every move of his graceful body says as plainly as any words, "I'm nowhere near as big as you, so I still feel like being careful. But though you are a giant you're pretty much of all right and I'm trusting you. What have you got in your pockets today?"

Now I think he is a bright squirrel because he was able to figure that all out for himself and so increase his own happiness. Where in the woods could he find a cookie or a peanut? All the nuts he gets from me and all he finds in the forest, which he does not eat immediately, he buries so that later on, when food gets scarce, he will have a good store put away. What good would it do for him to count them? He stores as many as he can, whatever the number, and does not need arithmetic. So why should I think him stupid just because he doesn't understand addition? A dull person may think he is smarter than a squirrel because he can count money to pay for food. He may not be able to improve himself though, or ever get a new idea through his head. But the squirrel, able to change its nervous little mind, is well rewarded and getting much more out of life.

Just for fun let us compare brighter human beings with a different chisel-tooth chap—a ground squirrel, say, the woodchuck. A woodchuck, for instance, does not think about orchestral music. But do most people, even those of us who go to concerts, think about the sound of a rain storm coming from far off, a million drops hitting a million forest leaves and the wind bringing it swiftly nearer, the sound growing ever louder till with a drenching roar it reaches a grand crescendo? The woodchuck listens to that, and if you have ever heard it you know it is as beautiful and exciting as any music ever written.

To the woodchuck orchestral music would be only puzzling noise. But the real storm is something he can certainly enjoy. Comfortably sitting near the door of his burrow he listens till the symphony is finished. Now the sun shines and out he comes into a glistening world to eat the freshened clover.

We want to be fair when we judge the minds of animals. Almost all of them know what they want and how to get it. How often we ourselves do not know those two important things! Always think, "What can an animal of this size and shape and nature enjoy in life? What does it need? And does it succeed in getting it?" Then you may judge that creature justly.

Well, now that we know what rodents are, how important they are in a world of other animals (including us), and how they differ from and how resemble ourselves, let us find out more about each special kind, here, there, and all the wide world over. The chisel-tooth tribe is such a big one we shall have to divide it up into families, each with its many cousins, close and not so close. The squirrel family is a good one to begin with.

2

TREE SQUIRRELS

YOU will be surprised to learn what a lot of different kinds of squirrels there are living in the world. We shall have to divide them into two big classes, according to their habits, to keep from getting them all mixed up. Suppose we call the classes tree squirrels and ground squirrels. Each squirrel belongs to one class, depending on where it chooses to make its home, in the trees or in burrows underground. One or more kinds of squirrels live in almost every part of the world except Australia.

In the tree class in our country are four main kinds— the little red squirrels, the larger gray squirrels, the still larger fox squirrels, and the little flying squirrels. Fox squirrels live in Pennsylvania and Ohio, all our southern states east of the Mississippi River, the very eastern part of Texas, and part of Mexico. East of the Mississippi one kind of gray squirrel lives both in the north and south, while other kinds of grays are found in far western states. Red squirrels and flying squirrels live in nearly all our states, Canada, and Alaska.

Tree squirrels generally have the finest, bushiest tails. I am not sure whether a squirrel is proud of his tail or not. He keeps it so well groomed and snaps it up and down so much one almost believes he wants it to be noticed. Whether this is so or not, were he to lose that tail he would become a much less spirited, spunky squirrel. He might really be downhearted. For, as with many other animals, a squirrel may feel about his tail as we do about our names. Many dogs and cats enjoy your stroking of their heads and bodies but object to any handling of their tails. Many people laugh at jokes on themselves but become angry if you joke about their names. You hurt their pride, and certainly tree squirrels have a right to take pride in that beautiful furry "feather" which they wear behind.

The tail is beautiful even when not moving, but when its owner scampers over the grass it follows his leaps in a wavy motion very graceful to behold. Each leap is half jump, half gallop, but the tail turns it all into long and lovely ripples. On tree trunks he still runs in the same way, seeming to go straight up or down as easily as he moves over level ground. High in the trees his tail must be very useful, helping him keep his balance as he springs from branch to branch and acting as a rudder as well as a parachute when he leaps from tree to tree.

Hunters tell me that the flicking of the bushy tail makes a squirrel troublesome to shoot. Some people think it also causes other enemies to miss their mark. Sometimes a hawk will swoop down from the air to snatch a squirrel from a treetop. It is always soaring about during the squirrel's busiest hours, from sun-up to mid-morning, from mid-afternoon till almost sunset. And while the squirrel takes a mid-day nap, climbing toward him may come a hunting animal called the marten, which steals up silently till near enough to spring. If the squirrel wakes in time, these enemies may only get a clawful or mouthful of tail fur as he leaps away.

Tails help many animals express themselves. Happy pigs' tails are tightly curled. Dismal pigs' tails hang down limply. Gay dogs wag their tails and hold them high. Doleful dogs carry them between their legs. Happy squirrels flick their tails in a contented way, but scared or angry squirrels flick them in a very different manner. An angry man may shake his fist and yell, "Get away from here!" A squirrel can jerk his tail up furiously each time he sput-

ters "Pfutt!" and mean the same thing. Perhaps tail-flicking keeps such a nervous animal from becoming *too* nervous, just as I seem to get along better as I write this book if I wiggle one foot or teeter in my chair.

Another grand use for a squirrel's tail is as a blanket. When sleeping he wraps it snugly about himself and keeps much warmer than ever he could without it. The tail and fur which protect a squirrel are a danger to him too at times. For hunters know the fur can be sold for making cozy wraps which people wear with the tails left on for ornament. The hunters also eat the squirrel meat and they say it has a pleasant flavor. What an animal eats makes a difference in how it tastes when in turn some other creature eats it. Fishes like suckers, which grub up rubbish at the bottom of a pond, taste rank compared to mackerel which catch shrimps and smaller fishes in the open sea. Pigs fed on garbage never make as good pork as those that root for nuts and acorns in the forest. These give to the pork a fine taste as they also do to squirrel meat pie, no doubt.

Where squirrels are not hunted they lose some of their fear of people and may become quite tame. In fact they sometimes grow too bold and the people who have befriended them and fed them have trouble for their kindness. As a boy I witnessed such a case when I went to visit in a beautiful suburb of Chicago, known as Evanston. It was a town full of fine houses set amidst tall oaks. Gray squirrels were chasing each other through all the trees and on every lawn there seemed to be at least a dozen. They paid little attention to the village dogs which were mostly muzzled anyway and not enjoying the "freedom of the city" as the rodents were.

Everything would have been all right if the squirrels had stayed on the lawn or in the trees, or even on the verandas, front and back. But they had decided that to live inside the people's houses would be grand. And being chisel-toothers they had gnawed holes through the roofs and set up housekeeping in nearly every attic. They dragged in bushels of oak leaves and left so many in the rain spouts that water couldn't get through and splashed all over in places where it wasn't wanted. Once inside the houses they studied their chiseling lessons well and practiced on everything in the attics, tearing open chests and boxes, spoiling many a nice old piece of furniture, and doing exactly as much damage as any gang of busy rats could do, or more. They rolled hard, noisy nuts and acorns over the attic floors or dropped them clattering through the hollow house walls, keeping people awake in bedrooms below. They chattered, scolded, and squealed.

They even went to church, going in through open doors and windows on hot summer Sundays. This was very disturbing. The preacher lost track of the good words he was saying. The organist lost track of the chords she was playing. The choir could scarcely go on with its songs. And the whole congregation had a terrible time just trying to pay attention. It must be hard to think about what you are doing when squirrels start racing over the organ pipes and choir loft railing, or under the pews and up and down the aisles.

In those days hardly anyone had ever seen an automobile. Many fine horses were kept by the residents of Evanston. The squirrels went into the stables and ate pecks and pecks of oats. They almost had to help themselves that way because the people had long since given up trying to feed their ever increasing numbers. The people did not seem to know just what to do. I never visited there again so I don't know what finally was done, but they surely needed a Pied Piper to lead their squirrels away to the woods.

Another thing those squirrels did was make life miserable for the birds. Squirrels like eggs as much as we do. But they don't keep hens. So they rob birds' nests whenever they get the chance. You see, even the vegetable-eating rodent can become a beast of prey when hungry, and eggs or baby birds are easy to be had. Generally a pair of birds can keep watch and drive one thief away. But where so many squirrels live they fairly own the trees, and no two birds can save their eggs from a dozen squirrels. While they are trying to peck the first robber, three others may be sitting around the nest as at a breakfast table, getting egg on their chins.

It is very bad to have no birds about to eat the grubs and insects which attack the trees and lawns. Squirrels eat some insects but birds catch them by the thousands. I think it would have been wise for the people of that town to stop being tender-hearted for a time and go to making squirrel furs and squirrel pies, until only a sensible number of their chisel-tooth companions were left. Does that sound like a cruel idea? It is not really. There never would have been too many if the people had not overfed them, adding large amounts of food for years to that which nature had provided. It is not nature's way to have so many animals of one kind in so small a place. In Evanston, by kindness, not by hunting, the people had thrown nature out of balance. Sooner or later, in wild places, starvation or sickness destroys most of the creatures which have multiplied too swiftly. And in tamer Evanston something had to be done. It would have been kinder to kill some of the squirrels suddenly than to let them all become sick and suffer, slowly dying.

Before our doctors learned how to prevent it, nature used to send terrible plagues of sickness upon the people living crowded in great cities, causing millions of them to die. For we are animals too, and nature tries to make us live according to her rules like all the others. But we have found ways now to keep the plagues away. So we can live by the millions in the cities and still keep well. And almost everywhere we go there are too many of us to suit wild animals. But back there in Evanston, things had become turned around. There were too many wild animals to suit the people, or for the animals' own good either.

It is pleasant, though, to have a few squirrels near your home, which you may count as friends. If you can coax a squirrel to hop into your lap to eat the things you bring for him, it is fun and in a way exciting. When he steps upon your knee his touch feels as though he were charged chock-full of electricity. And no doubt he is. He is one of the liveliest things on earth, a "live wire" of the animal world. He acts as though he had more energy than he can hold. He fairly vibrates with it when he touches you.

To make good friends with him you must of course have something to offer which he likes. He will not overcome his shyness unless he can get more than your friendship for it. No squirrel will take chances with a big strange animal like you unless he is coaxed. Not only must you offer him a goody, but you must take care to make no sudden move or sound. Talk to him in a quiet, soothing way if you wish, but do not make the "giddap-horse" sound with your pursed lips as so many people do. It is too much like some of his own nervous noises and is more likely to worry him than otherwise.

When he finally takes something from your hand it may be the first time in his life that he has done such a thing. He will be excited and may not be quite sure where to place his teeth. But if they touch your fingers do not jerk your hand away. Just keep it gentle and there will be no accident. Next time he will be more expert and he will know you next time too. The quieter you are the sooner he will trust you and the better you will succeed.

This is true in making friends with all wild things. Most of them are full of curiosity. If you go into the woods and sit perfectly still, before long wild creatures will appear which you never would see otherwise. Either they will look you over very thoroughly (and in the case of squirrels or chipmunks, give you a good scolding) or pay no attention to you at all. You can watch them go about their own affairs and learn more about them than you ever can by viewing them in cages. By studying animals this way and reading what is already known about them, you will have much interesting fun, and you may discover a great deal. You may find out facts which no one else has ever known before. That peculiar song you heard in the forest—what bird sings like that? If you can only see as well as hear the singer, you may find that the sound is not made by a bird at all. It may be the unknown song of some rodent! For probably many different kinds of rodents sing though not much is known about it yet. Red squirrels have a bubbling, trilling kind of song. Various kinds of mice sing long sweet trills and churrs. But much of our rodent music lesson is still unlearned.

Summer tree house. How it is made inside.

It is often very easy to locate the home of a tree squirrel, the summer home especially. In the crotches of tall trees look for a large ball of leaves and twigs. That will almost surely be some squirrel's summer home. It looks pretty rough on the outside but the materials are woven together so well that wind and rain do not enter. Inside it is lined with soft, shredded bark and moss, thin grasses, and sometimes even feathers. A hole on one side, just big enough to let the owner through, is the door. Once in a while a squirrel will roof over an empty hawk's nest, line it, and live comfortably in the deserted home of his old enemy. And though red squirrels are tree squirrels they often show that they rather like ground squirrel ideas. For they are likely to have a spare room in the ground under the roots of a favorite tree where nuts are stored and they can run for safety.

TREE SQUIRRELS

One squirrel may have several summer homes. But only one squirrel lives in each nest except when there are babies. Even then the father lives by himself. And as soon as the children are old enough they have to go out and build homes of their own. Mother tree squirrels generally have from eight to twelve babies a year, one litter born in March or April, and another family later in the summer.

At first the young ones are quite helpless, being blind and naked except for a thin fuzz on their tiny bodies. But in about four weeks they are all neatly dressed in good fur, scampering in and out of the nest, playing tag in their great home tree. Then in no time they are leaving mother, brother, and sister, to wander off alone and set up house-keeping. Those born in April will build summer homes first. Those born in August will more likely look for hollow trees or deserted woodpecker holes for nest sites. The winter homes are generally in such places. Soft, warm nests are made where a squirrel, curled up in his tail (his own wool blanket) can sleep with no worry about firewood, coal, or oil for stoves and furnaces.

When mild spells come in the wintertime, sleeping squirrels awake. Up they get to stretch and yawn. Then down to earth they go to hunt for the nuts they buried in the fall and summer. Sometimes we are told that tree squirrels store up heaps of nuts in hollow trees on which to live the winter through. We are taught that we should be like that—work hard and save our pennies and some day we'll be rich. But many tree squirrels are not very good at saving. They work hard, it is true, burying every nut they cannot eat right away. Often they bury much more food than they can use in a winter. This is good because when they come down to dig up a meal they cannot remember exactly where each nut is buried. They have to hunt until they find one. Half the time they find nuts that other squirrels buried, while other squirrels are probably eating theirs. Their sense of smell is very keen and by sniffing along over the snow they can locate a nut or pine cone buried in the ground below. Down they burrow and up they come to sit and feast on good provisions. The pheasants and partridges (wild chickens which scratch the ground like barnyard fowls) turn up nuts and peck them open for a meal. But many are never found again. These sprout and become new trees in time. So, though tree squirrels waste their work, the trees they accidentally plant will grow and some day bear more nuts to feed their great grandchildren and ourselves as well. Many is the nut you have eaten from a tree some squirrel caused to grow without intending to.

They always act as if they hope not to be noticed at their work, making a hole quickly, pushing in the nut, covering it with swift dabs of their hands, looking rapidly this way and that. If they weren't in such a hurry perhaps they could remember better later on. Some make better pantry stores than others. The little red squirrels generally do a bet-

Red squirrel's underground store room

ter job than the bigger gray ones. Besides nuts they save great stores of pine cones. Where cedars grow they cut thousands of twigs bearing unripe little cones, dropping them all over the ground, then taking them off to store in cool damp places. The cones do not dry and open as they would if allowed to ripen on the trees. They even pick mushrooms and hang them out on bushes to dry in the sun, then store them away.

Even when a gray squirrel collects a lot of nuts together in a special place, perhaps against a tree trunk under a few dead leaves, some little red squirrel is likely to find and steal them all. For a red squirrel is up and about even in the coldest weather, poking his nose into everybody else's business, stealing from any neighbors whose food supply he can discover—nuts, acorns, seeds from gray squirrels, chipmunks, and mice in winter; eggs from nests of birds in summertime; corn and apples from farmers in the fall. He cuts an apple stem with one snip of his chisel-teeth, drops it, runs down and carries it home. The seeds

he saves for winter eating. In early spring when sap begins to swell the topmost ends of maple trees, red squirrels eat them off with relish. Perhaps it is good to have a taste of fresh green salad once again. They also gnaw slight hollows on the upper side of maple branches. Here the sap collects and they may drink sweet water as often as they please. They are most able to take good care of themselves, though perhaps not as likely to become friendly with people as gray squirrels are.

Though rodents generally are timid, they do not fear each other. They are sometimes very quarrelsome amongst themselves and do some really ferocious fighting.

Red squirrels are just about the spunkiest and, though but half the size of gray ones, are much the better fighters. They are better at swearing too. There are plenty of enemies to practice on: other squirrels, hawks, owls, bluejays, crows, house cats, bobcats, pumas, raccoons, bears, dogs, wolves, foxes, martens, minks, weasels, people and so on.

TREE SQUIRRELS

Red Sciurus, the scurrilous squirrel (Sciurus is his scientific name), has whistling, sneezing, growling, and barking noises for swear words, and often he gets so excited while cursing that it sounds as though he were making all his different noises at once. I have put up with many a chisel-sharp cursing just trying to untangle one sound from another and still I cannot see how he does it. But I am sure, if I were small enough, any red squirrel would fight me and chase me out of his forest. When you see his footprints in the snow they look like double exclamation points !! !!. The marks and remarks he makes go together perfectly.

Sometimes the red squirrels raise so many young ones that there is not food enough for all in their own neck of the woods. So they move to a new place where the trees and berry bushes bear more nuts and fruit. If a colony of the big gray squirrels is already living there, they do not fight the little red invaders long but leave in terror, all of them, to seek new homes elsewhere. Then you may read in the paper of a big moving day amongst gray squirrels. Suddenly hundreds are seen where none had been before, not settling down to stay but moving on, even swimming rivers. In the water they try to hold their tails out. They are heavy weights to drag when wet. Just try swimming with a blanket tied to your back and you will see. Many a poor squirrel never reaches the further shore. Those that do, stop at last when far enough from their red relations to have peace in the family once again.

Of course, gray squirrels may move because their own supplies of food have gotten scarce. Their moving days do not amount to as much as they did two hundred years ago. Long before General Washington was fighting armies of British redcoats, pioneer farmers were losing battles against the chisel-tooth graycoats. Hundreds of thousands of them marched through the land ruining the corn and wheat fields as they went. The State of Pennsylvania offered threepence apiece for every one of the enemy killed, and 640,000 squirrels were shot and paid for. This sort of thing went on for many years, the squirrel armies always growing smaller, till now we have laws to protect them lest they all be killed, for no longer are they any trouble.

The red squirrels of England do not seem to be as spunky as our own. Several years ago some American gray squirrels were set free in English parks. They raised big families and (to everyone's surprise) spread rapidly, driving the little English red squirrels away. English people do not like this any better than we enjoy having English sparrows and starlings drive our own birds out.

Fox squirrels, the biggest of all our tree squirrels, sometimes weigh as much as three pounds. They are not as graceful as their lighter cousins, but can move swiftly enough when danger is near. If hunters seek them without the help of dogs, fox squirrels do not always leave the ground to hide in a tree. They may just run off through the woods and leave the hunter without any game. Of course, if there are dogs a squirrel has to take to the trees right away, where it hides in a knothole or a clump of leaves or just teases the hunter by keeping always on the other side of trunk or branches, moving whenever the hunter moves.

If hunters do not bother them, fox squirrels like to use the same tree for their home year after year. They never have a great tribal moving day as the gray squirrels sometimes do, staying all their lives within a few miles of the woods where they were born. They store up food in hollow logs and knotholes, and bury separate nuts in the ground as other tree squirrels do. And they make winter and summer nests. But because most fox squirrels live in our southern states they have a very fine material handy for nest lining which northern squirrels do not. It is the Spanish moss which hangs from the branches of southern trees, very soft and light but strong and springy, an excellent stuff to sleep on. Many a human being has made himself a comfortable bed in the forest with it. And many a mattress has been stuffed with this same good moss the fox squirrels use.

Fox squirrels are not all colored alike. Their bodies may be sooty black or very dark brown, a rusty yellow color, or a pale smoky gray. The rusty-colored ones may be fairly light on their backs but dark cinnamon color underneath. The pale slaty gray ones wear black caps. And all between these three styles are fox squirrel furs which may be somewhat smoky and somewhat rusty, or somewhat rusty and somewhat sooty.

Squirrels in different parts of the world have a great variety of colors and designs in their fur, all sorts of browns and reds, oranges, yellows, white and black. Sometimes a pure white squirrel will be born with pink eyes and ears like the white mice and rabbits you probably have seen. In our northwest the red squirrels have black tails. In England and Europe they have high tufts on their ears. In our southwest gray squirrels have tufted ears. They shed the tufts in spring and spend all summer growing new ones. In Mexico one kind of squirrel has a gray back and red abdomen, while in India live the largest squirrels in the world, their backs of glowing chestnut, their under sides bright yellow. There are any number of other styles in squirrel clothing.

TREE SQUIRRELS

All tree squirrels are amazing acrobats. Chasing each other or on treetop journeys through the forest, they make such long and dangerous-looking leaps, it is hard to see why their little muscles are not torn to bits when they land in a tangle of twigs many yards away. Sometimes, though very seldom, they miss their mark and fall. But even then they rarely seem to suffer injury, but run off as though nothing had happened. Sometimes they jump to

FOX SQUIRREL GATHERING SPANISH MOSS

Flying Squirrels' Aerial Coasting Party

the ground from a good height. Once, when I came suddenly from the house, I so startled a gray squirrel in the near-by cedar tree that instead of hiding in it, he made a choking noise and jumped from a branch twenty-five feet above the ground. He crashed down through some blackberry bushes but ran off to the woods apparently unscratched or otherwise hurt. Fox squirrels spread their legs when jumping to the ground from high branches. It may help some to slow their fall, but they need what the flying squirrels have to really do it properly.

For though they do not actually fly like birds and bats, flying squirrels do glide long distances through the air. This is possible because the skin on their sides is widened into a kind of cloak reaching from their wrists back to their ankles. Thus when they stretch their legs the opened cloak turns the whole squirrel into a combination parachute and glider. Leaping from a high tree they glide to the lower trunk of another a hundred feet or more away. For an animal whose body is only five inches long, that is a grand glide. As soon as they light upon the other tree they scramble to its top and take off again, perhaps back to the trunk of the tree they have just left. A dozen or more may keep this up for quite a while, gliding together just for the fun, a kind of aerial coasting party.

Flying squirrels live in almost all parts of our country. But they hardly ever come out of their nests until it is almost night, and so are seldom seen. For they are what

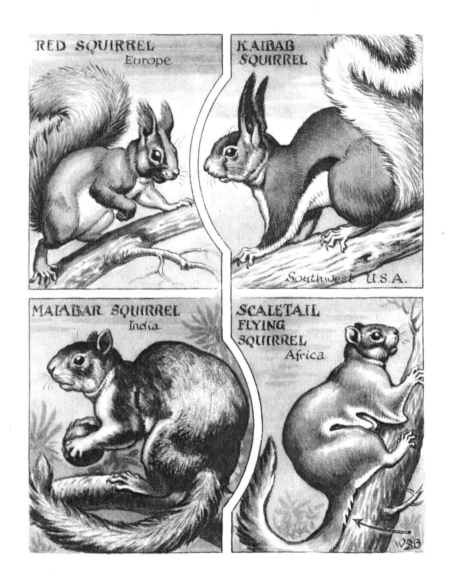

RED SQUIRREL
Europe

KAIBAB
SQUIRREL

Southwest U.S.A.

MALABAR SQUIRREL
India

SCALETAIL
FLYING
SQUIRREL
Africa

are called nocturnal animals, creatures which sleep all day and play and work only in the hours of darkness. Being very small they often make their homes in empty woodpecker holes. They eat small nuts and berries and many insects. They are the most sociable of all the squirrels and often break the general rule about living alone, especially in winter. At least fifty have been found living together in one old hollow tree. They make very charming pets, coming out of their nests in the evening, scampering about the house of their human friend, climbing his window curtains, gliding down, using him as a tree, hunting for goodies and even falling asleep in his coat pockets.

In India some flying squirrels are extremely large, being four feet long, counting the tail. In Africa the flying squirrels are known as scale-tails because of a row of hard stiff scales on their tails' undersides. It is an extra help for living in trees. When they sit upon a slanting limb or climb a tree trunk these scales catch on the bark and hold them up, like the ankle spurs worn by men at work on telephone poles.

3

GROUND SQUIRRELS: CHIPMUNKS

IN the ground squirrel class there are a great many different kinds, and of the different kinds there are still more and more varieties. Take chipmunks for instance. A chipmunk is just one kind of ground squirrel. But there are dozens of different kinds of chipmunks. And the ground squirrel class contains other rodents which hardly anyone thinks of as squirrels at all. Prairie dogs may "bark" but they are no more dogs than prairie schooners are ships. They are just simply squirrels, ground squirrels. And so are the woodchucks—big and heavy and slow, but squirrels just the same. Your eyebrows will go up when I tell you that beavers are squirrels, but it is true! We shall have to keep them in a class by themselves since they live neither in the trees nor the ground, but in the water. Beavers are water squirrels.

Ground squirrels live in most parts of the world except Australia. But of all ground squirrels in our country, the ones most people see the oftenest are the chipmunks. There are two main kinds, the eastern chipmunks and the western chipmunks. Texas and all the states straight up from there to Canada have hardly any chipmunks. These states separate the eastern and western chipmunks from each other and divide the country almost evenly between them.

It is not very easy for anyone but natural history scientists to tell most of the western from the eastern chipmunks. To most of us chipmunks are chipmunks and that is enough. All have shorter, less bushy tails and narrower heads than tree squirrels, perhaps because they live in tunnels underground. All have five dark stripes down their backs and several white ones. But for the most part western chipmunks are even more active than their lively eastern kin, and less shy. They have slightly longer tails, slimmer bodies, and finer stripes. But they vary in color from deep, heavy hues where forests are deep and heavy, to light tints in the more sunny, drier places. In northern Minnesota, Wisconsin, Michigan, and part of southern Canada, the eastern and western chipmunks meet and share the woods together. From there northward the western chipmunks

spread up through Canada clear to the Arctic Circle.

There are chipmunks in eastern Europe and all over northern Asia also. Think how many chipmunks altogether that must mean. Many millions of them scampering about all summer, digging homes beneath the ground, raising families and storing food for winter use, a grand lot of lively, beautiful little animals. But perhaps not as many in this country now as in olden times. Early settlers had almost as much trouble with chipmunks eating their crops as with gray squirrels. The government also paid a price for every chipmunk killed. Chipmunks migrate for food as do gray squirrels, and when hungry they will move in large numbers till food is found. If the food be a farmer's grain fields, so much the worse for him. They will cut off the heads of grain to eat and carry away. They dig up the corn he has just planted.

Unlike tree squirrels, a chipmunk has no special summer home amongst tree branches, though he can climb well enough if he cares to. Should he see a dog, for example, and be unable to reach his burrow in time to escape this enemy, he can scurry up a tree in jig time. Or once in a while he may climb nut trees and gather food like his tree squirrel cousins, though he never risks leaping from branch to branch and tree to tree as they do. As a rule western chipmunks climb more than their eastern relatives. But here in the Catskills an eastern chipmunk used to waste a lot of time in the alder bushes outside our house, trying to steal eggs from a catbird's nest ten feet above the ground. P.S. He never managed to do it.

Front door hidden by overhanging grass: no dirt heaped here · Pasture fence · Dirt in thick bushes around back door

HOW TO KEEP A SECRET

Most of a chipmunk's day is spent on or in the ground. He makes very neat, good burrows, and unless you see him going in and out you are not likely to know where the entrance is. For he doesn't make a pile of dirt outside as prairie dogs and woodchucks do. He keeps his hiding place as secret as he can. But how can he dig a tunnel without throwing out dirt? Well, he likes to live near old stone

48

walls, under fallen logs, stumps, brush piles, wood piles, rubbish piles, or banks where bushes grow. Some people say that he starts digging deep in the bushes where no one can see the dirt brought out and digs through till he comes out where he wants his doorway to be. Then he pushes the dirt back into his first opening amongst the bushes and blocks it up.

Others think he must carry dirt away in his pouches. His pouches are in his cheeks. They open inside his mouth between his chisel-teeth and chewers and reach clear back under his ears. He really has bags under his eyes. When full they do not make him look very handsome. He seems to have the mumps. They can be stretched and filled so full that his head becomes almost three times as wide as we expect to see it. Whether he ever uses his handy bags to

49

carry dirt we cannot say, but we do know how he most often uses them. He is a splendid storer-upper, better than the red squirrel. No matter how angry a farmer might be, he never would call the chipmunk who takes his grain a slouch. The scientists call him Tamias, which is a Greek word meaning storekeeper, not one who sells but one who saves food.

With his pouches he is better fitted for his work than tree squirrels are. Where a tree squirrel would have to make six trips to carry off six nuts, a chipmunk can carry all six at once—three in each cheek pouch plus one more in his mouth. He picks a nut up, opens his mouth and, with a swift push of his left hand, stuffs it into his right pouch. He stuffs the left pouch with his right hand. When his pockets are bulging, filled to the limit, he takes one more nut in his teeth and home he goes most mumpily. He can carry about one hundred and fifty grains of wheat at one time, seven or eight large acorns, or over two dozen kernels of corn, and so on with like amounts of whatever he happens to be gathering.

Chipmunks are very thrifty, for besides eating cherries they carry home the pips to be eaten as nuts in winter. They gather ripe berries of many kinds and various grass seeds besides the farmer's wheat and corn and buckwheat; also acorns, beech, hazel, hickory, and other nuts. If a nut is of a kind which has a sharp point on one end, the chipmunk carefully bites it off with his chisel-teeth before stuffing it into his cheek pouches. Thus he never gets any holes in his pockets.

Chipmunks also bury some food in shallow pits in the ground, as tree squirrels do, or under layers of fallen leaves. Whatever stores the chipmunks lay up squirrels will steal if they can find them. Though they work themselves, they are glad to profit by the chipmunk's work as well. The chipmunk is a better banker and sometimes tree squirrels are bank robbers. We should be told to work and save like chipmunks rather than like squirrels. Did you ever wonder what makes a chipmunk save up food, how he happens to have such a habit? It *is* a habit, and probably his ancient ancestors had to learn it. For habits can be learned, and the chipmunk's ancestors learned to save as we too can get the good habit of saving. He probably never thinks to himself as many people believe: "Hm! I'd better lay up a big supply this year. Looks like a long hard winter ahead!" He just practices his habit.

Perhaps this is how it all got started. Possibly the saving habit grew out of other habits the chipmunk ancestors had already. One habit all creatures have is seeking food. Everything must find a fairly steady supply of food or die. So every animal that lives has this most important first habit. For a little animal like a chipmunk there is a second most important habit. He must not only seek food; he must also seek a safe place to enjoy the food he finds. His world is full of danger. All his ancient relatives who did not learn this safety-seeking habit were killed and eaten by prowling enemies. They had no children to carry on their carelessness. But the chipmunk's great-grand-ancestor who had the safety-seeking habit, had many descendants, all just as careful as himself.

Where would this great-grand-ancestor feel and be most safe? Inside his own snug burrow, of course. So, more often than not, he toted his food home to eat it. In spring and summer he found just enough for daily needs. He would take a morsel home, eat it, and go out to look for more. But when autumn filled the world with ripe fruits and nuts and seeds, he could not eat half what he saw around him. But he already had this habit of picking up everything he could find and taking it home. And so much food everywhere rather excited him. He was like a boy looking at a pile of cookies. His eyes, perhaps, were bigger than his stomach. For just as the boy, after eating all the cookies he can, will carry one more off in his pocket, so the chipmunk's ancestor began carrying home all the nuts and seeds and things he could. There he might barely nibble on them, drop them, and go out for the fun of finding more and more. Without realizing it he was laying up a store.

Then came tough times—long, long winters perhaps. Only the ancient chipmunks who had accidentally stored up provisions, because they had both the food-seeking and safety-seeking habits, had anything to munch on as they waited for the far-off spring. The careless ones who were not killed and eaten in the summer time starved to death during the winter. Perhaps that is how chipmunks have got to be such good storekeepers. And of course, the ancestors who could stuff most into their mouths gathered the most food and lived best through long winters and had the strongest babies in the spring. Maybe it was only these who managed to live, the ones who were most like a boy who eats all the cookies he can, stuffs his mouth full, and puts more into his pockets. I wouldn't be surprised if that is how all chipmunks living today happen to have stretchy pockets in their cheeks.

The burrow home to which a chipmunk takes his food is generally a tunnel running down almost three feet below the ground and possibly ten to twenty feet long, depending somewhat on how many other chipmunks may be living

with him. For chipmunks keep house together, perhaps a half dozen or so calling the same burrow home, all helping to bring in the food they need for winter use. Near the far end of the tunnel is a cave-room, as big as a bushel basket sometimes, where a nest of leaves and dry grass rests on a large store of nuts and other food that keeps well. The main tunnel branches off to other rooms for smaller nests and storage chambers. The whole underground household is always clean and sweet, for the chipmunks also dig out a special room for a toilet.

All through the cold weather they live snugly under the snow and frozen top soil with everything they need to make them comfortable. They hibernate to some extent in the colder places where they live, but often awake to tidy up and eat of their stores. When the weather thaws a bit they come out and run about in the snowy sunshine. People say when they see this that the winter will soon be over, but it is no sign of anything except that chipmunks don't sleep all winter and like a bit of sunny fresh air whenever they can get it. When spring returns they add sweet new buds, dandelion blossoms, and so on to their fare. They catch a few small frogs and newts and snakes, and eat many beetles, caterpillars, and snails. They begin carrying home great loads of dry grass to make the nests up new. For baby chipmunks will soon be born. If the mother chipmunk can find soft feathers she will use them to line the nest. Her four, five, or six babies will be blind and without any fur at first, and feathers will keep them warm whenever she leaves the nest. Some day someone will find out for certain whether mother chipmunks raise more than one family a year. Though young chipmunks may be seen in a certain region in early summer and others later on may be seen in the same region, no one knows if the same mother has raised them all or not. This is a problem for future naturalists to solve; what becomes of the dirt where the burrows are dug is another one.

When you first meet a chipmunk you may only hear him. He will probably be looking straight at you from some safe shelter, uttering his sharp signal of danger, a loud "Tchip! r-r-r!" Indians first called him chipmunk or chipmuck, a name intended to imitate the sound no doubt. If you do come suddenly face to face with him he will do one of two things—run like mad for his burrow or freeze.

THE OLD FREEZING GAME

If he thinks he can make it, he will run with his little tail straight up in the air, chattering terrified squeals. But so great is his curiosity that almost before his tail disappears down the hole, out comes his face again to have a good safe look at you. Or before he runs, if he thinks you haven't seen him, he may play statue or freeze. Even so brightly marked an animal as he may not be noticed if he doesn't move. You can freeze too, and then it is a contest to see who gets tired first. Your stillness will gradually make him less nervous and presently he will make a dash for safety.

All wild animals know how to freeze, the beasts of prey and those they prey upon. Your pet cat knows all about it. If she sees a chipmunk first she freezes till its back is turned, sneaks closer, and freezes every time it moves, hoping to get close enough to spring before she is noticed.

But if the chipmunk sees the cat first it may freeze, hoping the cat will fail to see it. My brother once saw a chipmunk freeze when a young cat came suddenly around the corner of the house. But the cat had seen the chipmunk and was already close enough to spring, which she did. So the chipmunk ran toward its hole. But the cat moved faster and was nearly upon it when the chipmunk did a peculiar thing. It suddenly turned over on its back, feet in the air. The cat was surprised and hesitated. The chipmunk jumped up and ran a few steps, turning over again as the cat jumped after it. It did this several times till finally it darted down its burrow and didn't turn around for another look! The cat looked surprised and embarrassed.

Among the chipmunk's many enemies are hawks, big snakes, foxes, coyotes, badgers, and wildcats. But the worst enemy of all is the weasel. It is longer and stronger than a chipmunk but its legs are so short that it can go into any chipmunk burrow with ease. Here it can kill the whole family, which it does to satisfy its hungering thirst for blood. It is one danger from which the chipmunk cannot escape by running to its burrow. Indeed, the burrow is the very worst place to go when a weasel is about.

When not in danger and enjoying life, the chipmunk calls to his friends with a "chuck chuck" sound made down in his throat. And in spring when he feels extra happy to be out in the sunshine after the long winter, and it is time to seek a mate, he repeats this "chuck" so many times so rapidly that it becomes a chipmunk's song. On bright sunny days you will see the chipmunks oftenest and hear their calls. On dull days they may not even leave their homes, but when they do they are quieter and not so lively.

Thousands of squirrels of many kinds have been kept as pets. And very charming pets they often are. But some people claim that chipmunks never become as tame and friendly as, say, gray squirrels. I think that must depend very much on who takes care of them. Here is part of a letter I received from a girl who lives in Georgia, which will show you what I mean. Notice how she wins her "Chipie's" trust, how she studies his wishes. And see how the chipmunk, because of her careful sympathy, learns to do all manner of things that other chipmunks never do, having many odd adventures which he thoroughly enjoys. To him she must seem a very lively, lovely creature-tree from whose gentle branches he receives the most delicious things to eat. Here is the letter:

"Chipie was caught by a cat. I rescued him and brought him in the house half dead about the fifth of September. I put Chipie in some nice warm cotton and gave him some milk out of an eye dropper. Ever since then he has made an ideal pet. Chipie is now nine months old.

"After Chipie had gotten quite tame I began to feed him different things to see what he would eat and everything I gave him he ate except eggplant, spinach, beets, and carrots. He even drinks Coca-Cola. There is one thing

Chipie likes best and that is candy. Chipie also likes ice cream, his favorite being chocolate. One day I fed him some steak and he liked it very much. His usual diet is milk or orange juice, nuts, meat, and one vegetable. For dessert he has candy, cake, or ice cream. I feed him three times a day; at lunch time his meal is very light.

"The shoe repair man made a harness specially for Chipie. It was lots of fun to have Chip measured, his neck is three inches and his body four inches. In all Chip has had two harnesses made. The harness has a shoestring to lead him by. In the picture you were speaking of I suppose you noticed Chipie's short tail. Well, Chipie loved to get in all sorts of cracks, so one day while he was exploring the radiator his tail got caught; when he pulled his tail trying to get loose half of it came off in the radiator.

"These are some of the experiences I have had with Chipie: about two weeks ago Chipie was gnawing the wires in his cage (which is a special squirrel cage from California) so I decided to let him out to run around in the house. For about two hours he was running and playing. Then I missed him and I couldn't find him so we just let him play while we went on to bed. Next morning daddy said he had felt something run across his feet that night. I looked under the cover and there was Chipie all nice and warm. That was where he had spent the night.

"I have a Boston bulldog who is about ten years old. His name is Chick. He and Chipie are fast friends. Chipie lets Chick ride him on his back. They both enjoy it.

"Chipie loves to play. He will get on the rug and turn over and over. If you wiggle your finger at him he will squeak. When he gets scared he makes a shrill whistle.

"Some time ago Chipie went down in the basement. I did not know where he was but I soon thought that he might have gotten down there so I went down and called him. He came out black and dirty. I gave him a bath even if it wasn't Saturday night.

"Chipie has a bath every Saturday night. Of course he does not like the water so much but he does like to keep clean. After the bath Chipie is wrapped in three bath towels to keep warm.

"Chipie has a very strange habit. He likes to ride in the car. One day I took him into a store riding on my shoulder. Everyone turned around and stared at him. I have never had so many questions asked me at one time in all my life. But it was lots of fun.

"Another one of Chipie's favorite sports is to sit on the piano while I am playing. Once or twice he would jump down on the keys and run up and down the piano striking the different notes as he passed. At times if Chipie is hungry and is lost in the house, if I play my piano he will come to me.

"I hope you have gotten the information you needed and for any person who likes pets I recommend a pet chipmunk."

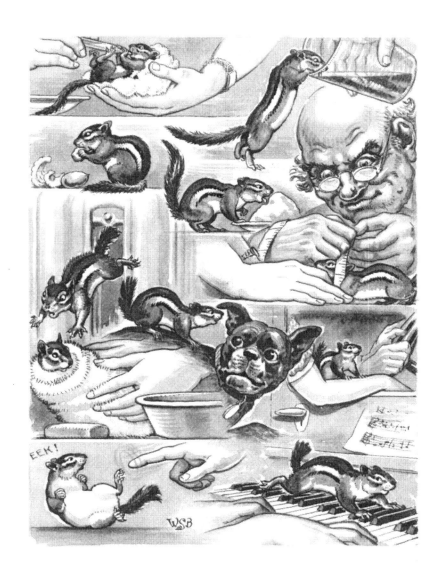

SPERMOPHILE BOWLER'S CLUB

4

GROUND SQUIRRELS:
SPERMOPHILES

LIVING almost everywhere that chipmunks do, as well as on the open prairies and in desert places where no chipmunks live, are other ground squirrels which might be called the tenpin type. They have a freezing habit which makes them look like tenpins, standing straight and stiff with hands held close against them while they watch and listen for expected trouble.

Because they live in colonies making miles of tunnels underground, as gophers also do, many people call these tenpin squirrels gophers. But that is wrong, as you will see when we come to gophers. These tenpin ground squirrels are really Spermophiles, a scientific name which means seed lovers. For they live on seeds more than anything else, especially out on the treeless prairies where there are no nuts and very few berries. They carry home in their cheek pouches a great many seeds to store away but only for use in the early spring when they wake from their long winter sleep and there is nothing to be found worth eating in the cold, wet, melting world outside.

For in the colder places where they live, spermophiles hibernate, getting very fat each fall, going to bed sometimes even before cold weather comes, and waking months later, lean and much in need of breakfast. The waking up must be not altogether pleasant. I should think it might be like at least two feelings that we know combined. Have your fingers or toes ever come so near to freezing that they were numb and hardly hurt? Do you remember the pain when you thawed them out? How would you like to be like that all over? And of course you know how much you feel like groaning when your arm or leg has gone to sleep and is coming to again. What if your entire body felt that way? For the hibernating squirrel is as cold as your all but frozen hand. And his blood flows through his body even more slowly than yours moves in your sleeping leg.

But probably during the worst part of the waking the squirrel is still too sleepy to realize much of anything. At worst it may be like a very bad dream. He has to wake up slowly from such long sleep. The waking makes him tremble from head to foot. His head shakes violently, then he thaws out through his shoulders and arms, then down his back and hind legs. Finally he yawns and stretches, and though his eyes still are dull and heavy he knows one

thing for certain, he is hungry.

So after a dry breakfast on some of his stored up cereal he goes up and out for a nibble at the first tender shoots of new green grass, spring tonic. He goes out almost as gradually as he awakes. Slowly, moment by moment his head comes out a little. He waits, watching the sky for hunting hawks, listening and sniffing the air for the sign of a fox about, or other enemy. Bit by bit he comes clear out. At first he does not go far from his burrow. One cannot scurry back to safety fast enough on thin and weakened muscles.

Before many days he is feeling fit as ever, even fitter, and starts looking about his world for a little lady spermophile to be his mate. He leaves his own burrow and moves into hers, and after a while there is a set of brand-new living tenpins in the nest. There may be ten, for some spermophiles have all the way from five to over a dozen babies at a time. With so many babies to look after, the mother squirrel becomes very impatient with the father. He is only

in the way as far as she is concerned. He cannot help care for the babies and though he did dig out wider places in their tunnels to make passing easier, somehow it just seems to her that he is always getting under foot. So at last he goes off a little way and digs himself a new burrow where he can be near at hand but not be scolded all the time. Very sensible of him, don't you think?

The babies will live with their mother till nearly full grown. Then while there is still time to put on plenty of fat, to dig good burrows, and lay up a few rations, they move out and set up housekeeping in their own separate homes. Other families close by are doing the same and a great ground squirrel town or colony appears. And so another winter comes and each one sleeps, to wake and mate and raise more youngsters. If food is plentiful the squirrels become very numerous, as many a farmer can tell you to his sorrow.

Some of the spermophile ground squirrels have very beautiful fur. One of the most beautiful is like an eastern chipmunk, only very much larger, whose colors have all been brightened, the stripes fewer but wider and more distinct, the ruddy head, shoulders, and back turned to a glowing orange-yellow. Naturally he is called by many people Big Chipmunk, or Golden Chipmunk, or Golden Mantled Chipmunk. He isn't a chipmunk, though, but a Golden Mantled Spermophile Ground Squirrel. If you think that is too long a name just look at his scientific one —*Callospermophilus lateralis chrysodeirus!* In Oregon, where his colors are the finest, people call him Calico Squirrel, which seems to me a very good name.

Golden Chipmunks or Calico Squirrels can be seen in our western states all the way from Canada into the mountains of northern Mexico. They live too far west ever to meet any eastern chipmunks, but often live among western chipmunks. You can always tell them from chipmunks by their brighter, broader colors, much greater size and slower movements. They are inclined to be fat even in midsummer, but are very fat indeed in autumn, because, unlike chipmunks, they hibernate for full five months or so. Another somewhat unchipmunky habit is the long sun bath habit. Like other spermophiles, the Calico Squirrel loves to lie for hours on pleasant summer days on top of a stump or stone or little hill, not far from his burrow, not asleep but quietly watching everything that goes on about him. The stump or stone or hillock is his theatre seat whence he can view the passing show. Sometimes, if he thinks some danger may be near, he takes the tenpin pose and holds it steadily, bolt upright, very still but very wide

awake. He dare not sleep there, for a hawk, fox, coyote, bobcat, snake, or weasel would surely catch him napping. He must always see them first and dash down his hole.

Often he has several holes leading into his burrow which he digs in the same sort of places that a chipmunk chooses. Like the chipmunks, Calico Squirrels carry their tails high when running and are likely to stay indoors on dull days. Being fond of sunshine, they like open places in the forest and come to live about any camp or cabin, digging homes under the buildings and stealing whatever food they can from the people. They are grain robbers when they live near farms, stealing it both from the field and barns. Of course they carry home heaps of other seeds and such fare in their cheek pouches as real chipmunks do, storing them away underground to use on rainy days. Where sheep are raised they line their nests with tufts of wool the sheep lose passing through thorny brush. In this cozy bed they sleep the winter months away, only using the stored up food when waking in the spring.

The Thirteen Striped ground squirrels are also beautifully marked. The name "thirteen striped" may mislead you. If we consider them to be dark brown squirrels, they have about seven light buff stripes down their backs. If we consider them light buff squirrels, they have about six dark brown stripes down their backs, each brown stripe containing a row of buff-colored spots. The namers of these chisel-tooth chaps considered them to be all stripes, thus counting thirteen. And so actually they are both striped and spotted at the same time. This elaborate uniform is even more useful than ornamental, for it disguises them in the grass of the prairies where most of them live. I have seen them in the forests of northern Wisconsin and even there their markings helped disguise them, especially in the brush amongst the roots of giant yellow birch trees. They shared these woods with eastern and western chipmunks and red squirrels and were much more cautious in their comings and goings about our camp than their

" 'nother mess to clean up"

spunky relatives.

But in dealing with these relatives and amongst themselves, they are often very short-tempered and given to fighting. They might almost be called bloodthirsty. They even have a weasel-like form, being longer of body than other squirrels. They do kill other squirrels sometimes and eat them. They catch field mice and, once in a while, young chickens and turkeys when living close to farms. They eat many insects, and in summer when grasshoppers and caterpillars are plentiful, they seem to forget their seed-loving tastes and live entirely on insect meat. In the old days when great herds of buffalo roamed the plains and prairies, and some of our foolish, wasteful ancestors went around shooting them by the thousands just for fun, these meat-eating seed-lovers used to eat all the great dead animals left lying where they fell.

It is said that oftentimes if two thirteen stripers are put into a cage together they fight till one is killed. When this is so they do not make very good pets, of course. But in a pet shop I have seen six living peacefully in the same cage. They had even made up a very good game to play together

READY? GO! uphill work team work WHEE!

THE ONE RING ~ THIRTEEN STRIPER CIRCUS

on their exercise wheel. One squirrel would get inside it while another would get on top of it. The one inside sat very still gripping the little wire treads firmly with all four feet. Then the chap on the outside, holding fast to one side of the cage with one hind foot, gave a quick pull on the wheel with his other three. This got the wheel to whirling. Instantly he would let go the side of the cage and run like mad on the topside of the wheel, giving the chap inside it a dizzy ride. Sometimes the running squirrel would slip down between the whirling wheel and the side of the cage. Then it was very hard exercise, like running up a ladder, but never would he stop until he missed his footing. Often he climbed back atop the wheel immediately and gave his friend spin after spin. When this was not going on two others would run together within the wheel, one facing upward, one downward, or side by side. Perhaps this jolly cageful was a mother and her almost grown-up children. The man in the shop could not tell me. He was a very bad naturalist, not only calling them chipmunks but flying squirrels!

During all their play they never made a sound, but out on the prairie such ground squirrels call to each other with chirps and trilling whistles. When you approach one of their widespread colonies every squirrel whistles warning to all the others in a great trilling concert, the noise even coming from underground as they dart down their burrows. The colony may cover acres and acres of land, but, like the chipmunks, these squirrels show no dirt from their diggings amongst the grasses. However, you can readily know where the burrows are, for, also like the chipmunks, they must turn around and pop their heads out for a look.

Many other spermophile ground squirrels, much like the thirteen stripers, though wearing far less fancy uniforms, live in the prairie and desert parts of our country. It would

Antelope "Chipmunk"

WSB

California Ground Squirrel

be impossible to describe them all in this book. But we must mention several more. Another, also incorrectly called chipmunk, is the antelope ground squirrel. No doubt it is called chipmunk because it is small and has a stripe on each side. And it is called antelope because it carries its little white tail curved up over its rump when running, somewhat like an antelope.

The burrows are often dug under a protecting cactus, sometimes showing a pile of dirt beside the entrance, sometimes not. In some colonies these squirrels show little fear of people and gather where men are camping to pick up grain spilt when the horses are being fed. When they set up colonies near farms they make much trouble, digging up newly planted grain and stealing more when the crops have grown.

But even more troublesome is another kind of spermophile very common in California. The California ground squirrels, unlike other ground squirrels, have big and bushy tails. Any gray tree squirrel could take pride in wearing one. But their colonizing habits are more like prairie dogs. They never conceal their burrows, heaping the dirt up in a mound about the doorway. There they may sit in some safety. But they have a new enemy which they do not understand, and which kills them by the thousands now— poison.

Until a few years ago the farmers of California were losing at least twenty million dollars a year because of these squirrels. They have had to get rid of the enormous numbers that were feeding on everything they grew. It is much more serious than the trouble kindhearted people used to have in Evanston with gray tree squirrels. For besides all the wild seeds they enjoy, these bushy-tailed burglars gobble up a fifth of all the crops, tons and tons of wheat and other grain, alfalfa, and all such fruit as peaches, apricots, grapes, and prunes, as well as almonds.

Nobody can blame a squirrel for helping himself from the farmer's crops. He doesn't know anything about property. "Take whatever you can but don't get caught" is the only rule he knows. The farmers kill off the squirrels' enemies and at the same time provide better food and much more of it than ever the squirrels knew before. Naturally they eat better and raise bigger families. So the farmer has to begin taking the places of all these wolves, coyotes, foxes, badgers, weasels, wildcats, hawks, and eagles that he killed. No one kills golden eagles in California any more. They are needed to help the farmers fight the squirrels.

Ground squirrels give farms and ranches trouble in another way sometimes, especially where they dig in loose and sandy soil. Everywhere beneath the surface wind their tunnels. Many a galloping horse has suddenly sunk through into the burrows, breaking a leg. It is expensive losing good horses down squirrel holes. The same thing happens to cattle. No wonder the men are trying to get rid of the squirrels. But down on the west coast of Mexico live some Indians who consider certain long-tailed ground squirrels the best of friends. Their home is a big island not far from the mainland, called Tiburon. Much of it is rocky but much is a flat and sandy desert. All of it is very dry except for a few springs of water in its rocky hills, the places kept a secret by the Indians. They are a very savage people who have been at war with other Indians on the mainland and with all the white man's governments in

Mexico for hundreds of years. They sneak over to the mainland to steal livestock and often to kill people. This seems quite right to them. Their religion tells them that anyone outside the tribe is an enemy. A young man cannot marry before he has killed at least one enemy. So he commits a murder on the mainland.

Missionaries have never been able to teach them any

better. And many a force of Mexican soldiers has been sent to the island to rid the world of them all forever. But they are still there. And here is why: these savages kill and eat raw every animal of the land, sea, and air they can catch, except one. They never harm the ground squirrels which dig endless tunnels for miles and miles along their island shores. The soldiers have to bring their own water on mules. They cannot chase the swift-footed Indians without horses. And sooner or later the mules and horses always crash to earth, their legs buried and broken in the sand. After the unsuccessful soldiers go away the savages feast on the dead animals left behind. So there is one place at least where people and great colonies of ground squirrels get along together very well.

5

PRAIRIE DOGS

PRAIRIE dogs! Of course they are not dogs as any-one can see. But they bark very much like small and peevish Pomeranians, and so received their name. In habits they are much like spermophiles, but in size and figure more like woodchucks. A big fellow may weigh three pounds and stand more than one foot high, tenpin pose. They are naturally plump even in midsummer, but in the fall they are roly-poly just before they hibernate. Their tunnels have to be at least four inches wide or more. The entrances are still wider, flaring out like funnels in the piled up dirt. Sometimes badgers, big heavy-set cousins of the weasels, come and dig them even wider to get the prairie dogs within.

These holes offer just as much danger to the legs of cattle and horses as do the tunnelings of spermophiles. And these pudgy diggers also give their share of trouble to the farmers and ranchmen of the western plains. For, besides using what they please of his grain and alfalfa, they are the great grass eaters. Their colonies spread over hundreds of square miles in some places. And over all that range they eat much of the grass that men want for their cattle. Two hundred and fifty prairie dogs eat as much grass in a year as a cow. And there are millions of prairie dogs.

Prairie dog "towns" are not laid out in streets, but the homes of the little "people" are scattered all about, each burrow a few yards from the next. Between and all about the burrows the grass is kept cut short. For this reason it is hard for an enemy to creep up close without being seen. For though most of the neighbors may be visiting each other or busily nibbling grass, some always sit up tenpin style on the mounds of dirt about their doors, watching. When they see anything suspicious, such as a movement in the long grass at the edge of town, they bark loud warning, their stubby tails quivering with excitement. Everybody stops whatever they are doing to run for their holes. If prairie dog children try to go right on playing, their mothers rush at them barking frantically, and shoo them home. By this time everyone is barking by his doorway, ready to dive out of sight the minute the enemy appears.

Perhaps the movement in the grass was caused by a hungry fox. He knows that if he lies perfectly still, before long the whole town will forget their scare and perhaps one not too cautious prairie dog will wander near enough to be caught. If the enemy were a bird of prey swooping down, nobody would stand staring and barking at his door, but would dive out of sight instantly, chattering with vexation. Perhaps no one would show his head again for an hour or so. Just below the entrance to the burrow, prairie dogs dig a little side room in which to listen and from which they can be heard chattering angry ground squirrel curses at whoever spoils their day.

Not only do they have unwelcome visitors like hawks and foxes, but many prairie dog towns have uninvited guests who never know when it is time to leave. They are

rattlesnakes and little burrowing owls. It used to be supposed that they got along peaceably with their prairie dog hosts, but this is not so at all. The owls should be called borrowing, not burrowing. For though they live in burrows, they borrow them from the prairie dogs who dug them. And the rattlesnakes not only borrow a burrow to live in by killing and eating whoever lives there, but they go visiting amongst the neighbors, "the better to eat them" there, my dears. But sometimes they go into a burrow and never come out. Sometimes when the prairie dogs see a rattler go down a hole they rush and fill it up with dirt. The snake is buried alive!

Bad as the snakes are, that other awful bogeyman of ground squirrels, the weasel, is probably far worse. For he does not catch one squirrel and eat it. He kills a whole family just to suck their blood, the worst animal villain of them all. Then too, there are those other enemies—the men. Indians have always hunted prairie dogs for food, and later came white men wanting the grass for their cattle and setting poisoned goodies out to lure the prairie dogs to death.

In spite of all such worries they are, for the most part, very happy little animals. And if all goes well, the four or five babies born to each mother in the spring will grow rapidly, and by the time they are as big as chipmunks, will come out of their burrow for their first look at the very wide prairie world. Without any help they will learn to wrestle and play tag and to cut off bits of grass with their baby chisel-teeth. But they must be taught that the world is a dangerous place to play in. They do not understand the warning barks of grown-ups and must be taught to be afraid and dive down holes. When about half grown they pick out places for their own new burrows in which to spend the winter—often quite a distance from the town where they were born.

People used to think that prairie dogs made colonies in land where water could be reached by digging. They thought the burrows must go down that far. Otherwise how could the prairie dogs live in such dry places? Men who wanted to build ranch houses on the plains would sink deep wells in prairie dog towns. But never a drop of water did they find. The fact is that many rodents can get along with drinking little or no water. This is because their digestion is able to turn the starch in their food into water. And there is some water in the greens they eat, and when there is dew, that helps as well. It seems strange that a prairie dog can get water out of dry grass seeds or grain, but it is so; else how could a mother prairie dog give milk enough to raise five hungry babies?

6

WOODCHUCKS

LONG before any white men came to America, the Indians had named the animals. When the Englishmen arrived, they sometimes misunderstood the Indian names and used an English word which sounded something like it. This turned out to be rather silly in the case of "woodchuck" which in England is a name for a bird, the green woodpecker. The English heard some tribes call the big American ground squirrel "otchock," while others called it "wee-jack." The sound reminded them of "woodchuck," so that became the wee-jack's English name.

Such a name doesn't mean a thing. Chuck means to chuckle, to cluck like a chicken, to pat, and to toss a short distance. But woodchucks never chuckle no matter how happy, they never sound like broody hens, they don't go around patting wood or tossing it about. There used to be a song which started, "How much wood would a woodchuck chuck if a woodchuck would chuck wood?" But it won't.

The woodchuck's other English name is ground hog, which doesn't mean much either. It may live in the ground and grow fat, but it is certainly no hog. Other animals share this name. The very first animal, almost the first word in any good dictionary, is the aardvark. That is a Dutch name meaning earth pig. But it is given to a very strange-looking animal not related to pigs or rodents either.

Neither is the fat grub of the June bug or May beetle which lives in the ground and is also called ground hog sometimes.

Ground-Hog Day

Of course you know about ground-hog day. And I hope you know that that too is a lot of nonsense. It comes on the second of February. The woodchuck or ground hog has been fast asleep, hibernating, since way back in October. People are wishing for spring and many believe that the ground hog, also wishing for spring, gets out of bed and comes out of his burrow to see how soon spring may be expected. They think that if there is bright sunshine and the ground hog sees his shadow, he goes back to bed again, knowing that there will be six more weeks of stormy weather before spring comes to stay. Really, no woodchuck ever opens an eye in early February. They do not know about ground-hog day. And suppose they did? Suppose every ground hog came out and took a good long look at the world? Would they all prophesy alike? Some

86

would see their shadows and others, where no sun was shining, would not. So some supposedly would say, "Winter for six more weeks," while others would say, "Spring'll be here any minute." And you might as well not listen to any prophets when they disagree.

Sometimes the woodchuck is called the whistler because the strong, clear note he makes so often sounds like whistling. But it isn't. When I was a boy many of my friends could whistle very loudly and shrilly and be heard a half mile away. My whistling was not strong but I could make as shrill a noise that carried just as far the way the woodchuck does it, with his vocal cords, his voice. So whistler is no better a name than ground hog.

The scientists' name for woodchuck is *Arctomys*. *Arctos* is Greek for bear and *mus* is Latin for mouse. Put together, *Arctomys,* they mean bear-mouse, which in a way describes the woodchuck's looks. His fur is grizzly, and he hibernates as bears do. Perhaps the best name of all is marmot, the name of that branch of the squirrel family to which woodchucks belong. We have marmots in our western states and others live in parts of Europe and in Asia. They are the biggest, heaviest ground squirrels of all, old granddaddies standing nearly three feet high tenpin fashion. The marmots of Europe and Asia live in bleak and barren places and form big colonies, somewhat as do our prairie dogs. But for the most part our western marmots, and especially our eastern woodchucks, are not so fond of company and do not live in colonies.

Each woodchuck has its own burrow which it digs near open fields where plenty of clover and other good blossoms and seeds are to be had. The burrow has one big main door about which the dug out dirt is piled and which anyone, person or animal, can easily see. But there are always one or two back-door ways at the other end of the tunnel. These are hard to see for they are hidden amongst rocks or rubble. The nest is somewhere under the rocks and this protects many a woodchuck and western marmot when bears come to dig them out.

Dogs try to dig them out too but this does not worry the woodchuck so much. The tunnel is long and the dog generally works on the main entrance, a long way from the nest and secret exits. Indeed many a time a woodchuck has lain flat on top of a rock, restfully frozen near its secret exit, and watched a dog twenty or thirty feet away wear himself out with useless digging. Some dogs are more of a worry than others. Dachshunds with their very short legs can get clear into a big woodchuck's burrow. That means trouble. Sometimes the dog catches the woodchuck, but sometimes he backs out yelping "Ki-yi" with old chuck's chisel-teeth gnawing his nose!

In the very early spring there may be other unwished-for visitors in the den. A fox, rabbit, or skunk sometimes uses a spare room in the burrow all winter while the woodchuck sleeps. If he wakes up cross and hungry to find such

The Warning

animals in his house, the chuck is very peevish about it and tries to put them out. He is so quarrelsome at this time of the year that he very often succeeds. The male woodchuck, out searching for a mate in spring, will fight with any other buck chuck he may meet. When he finally meets his mate they move either into his or her burrow and hollow out several extra nest rooms to accommodate a large family.

Some time in April from three to seven babies are born, and in a month or a little more these youngsters are big enough to come out and play and learn to nibble. They have to learn to run inside when mother whistles warning, and they learn to freeze when they hear the danger signals of other creatures. When the crow or bluejay or the partridge calls in a certain way, they freeze as often as not, just to be on the safe side. They learn to come out of the burrow very slowly, and to go back tail first with the same slowness. This they do when the enemy they spy has not seen them. Otherwise it is a dive in head first.

Besides seeds and blossoms, woodchucks like vegetables. They get into gardens and do much damage. The netting of our garden fence is set almost a foot underground to prevent woodchucks (as well as rabbits and porcupines) from getting in. They could dig under, of course, but up till now it has looked like too much bother to them. In the fall they steal apples and corn and eat for all they are worth to be fat and ready for the long winter sleep. Sometimes the farmer, pestered all summer and fall, finally raises up his gun and shoots the woodchuck. Indians on the Pacific coast shoot the woodchuck's western marmot kin, make warm robes of the fur, and eat the meat. Not many white people eat woodchucks. But I have, and though the meat is fat it has a good flavor, just as good as squirrel or rabbit, even better perhaps. Last year I read in the paper that there were many more woodchucks in Vermont than usual. They were doing more harm than usual too, and the farmers had to shoot many hundreds which their wives canned for the winter meat supply. One farmer's wife put up three hundred quarts.

That was the end of a good many ground squirrels and this is the end of the ground squirrel chapters. There is only one more kind of squirrel to tell about. Of all chisel-toothers he is perhaps the most wonderful, because of the way he lives and the great things he can do with his chisel-teeth. He is the water squirrel, the astonishing beaver.

7

BEAVERS

BEAVERS are next to the biggest rodents in all the world. Only the capybaras of South America are larger. In North America, from Alaska to Mexico, no other chisel-toothers are anywhere near as large and heavy. They are from forty to fifty inches long, counting their tails, and weigh from thirty to seventy pounds or more. But it is not their size that is so remarkable. It is the wondrous work they do, for no other members of the chisel-tooth tribe make such marvelous use of their tools as the beavers. They are the great lumberjacks of the rodent world, cutting down trees with their chisels more neatly than many a man can do it with an ax.

And no other rodents build so mightily, nor any other animal in the world (except man) for that matter. The trees are used not only as food but as part of the materials with which they build themselves snug cabins and great dams which deepen streams and hold back tons and tons of water. For to beavers plenty of deep quiet water is almost as important as air. In it they are fitted perfectly to live.

The Bank Home

When swimming under water, a beaver moves along smoothly and swiftly, paddling with his large hind feet which are as webbed as a duck's. His front feet, which are not webbed, he holds close to his chest. He sees very well under water and his fur-lined ears and his nostrils close very tightly. No water passes down his throat by accident. The fur-lined folds behind his chisel-teeth, which keep out splinters when he gnaws, keep out water just as well. His skin, covered with dense, brown fur under a coating of long coarse hairs, keeps perfectly dry. With his hairless, broad, flat, scaly paddle tail he steers. The tail may be

moved up and down like a whale's, increasing his speed or helping him to rise or swim deeper. If the beaver is frightened while swimming at the surface, he raises it out of water and brings it down with a loud thwack. This not only warns other beavers that an enemy is near, but gives him a quick start down out of sight to safety under water. The tail is a brace against which he leans while standing on his hind legs to gnaw down trees. And it helps him keep his balance while carrying loads on land, such as heavy branches or armfuls of mud.

The mud, with sod and stones, is used in building dams. When a pair of beavers seeks a suitable spot along some stream in which to make their home and start a colony, they look for a place where the banks are not steep and are covered with trees like poplars, birches, wild cherries, willows, and so on. The bark, twigs, and leaves of these

94

will furnish most of their food, while the branches and trunks will be used to build the dam and home cabin.

But first they make a temporary home where they can live until their dam and cabin are complete. They make a burrow in the stream bank which they start under water, digging it up through the land till it ends near the surface under the strong roots of a large tree. Here they hollow out a room and open a few air holes in its ceiling between the tree roots. Here too they are above the level of the water and will be even when it rises as they raise their dam.

The dam must be made in summer while the waters are flowing more gently than they do in spring. It is started in midstream and built towards both banks. The beavers bring branches and fasten them to the shallow bottom with mud and stones, the heavy butt ends facing up the current. They scoop up armfuls of mud or tear up heavy pieces of sod from the bank and push them in among and on the branches. They move stones that sometimes weigh ten pounds or more, and place them on the growing heap. By the time they have put down branches all across with mud and stones and sod, the stream will rise a few inches as its water is held back. The dam must be so well made and strong that the heavy ice of winter cannot break it, nor the rushing torrents of spring carry it away.

With crunching chisel-teeth, trees four or five inches thick are cut down along the banks. The branches are then bitten off close to the trunks, and dragged or carried into the water where they are floated down to the building dam. More armfuls of mud are scooped from the bottom behind the dam and are added with more stones and sod. The beavers are able to swim under water with these heavy materials held under their chins. Things are lighter under water and the beavers can move loads this way which they could scarcely stagger with on land.

You can see in the pictures how they handle the heavy tree trunks after cutting them into sections. The heavier

ways of moving logs to water

97

the trunk, the shorter they make the sections so that they never weigh too much to manage. Once in the water they are swum to the dam, a beaver holding the forward end in his teeth, his tail held hard over like the rudder of a tugboat towing a heavy ship. Steadily rises the dam with much mud plastered on its inner upstream side. And steadily rises the collecting water till it flows over evenly through the mesh of twigs and branches along the dam's entire rim, then onward down the valley.

The rising water spreads over its low banks back of the dam, making a big pond and perhaps many smaller ones with lots of swampy places all about. Then for some time the beavers do not have the hard work of moving felled trees to the water. They have moved the water to the trees. The pond must be so deep that no winter however cold can freeze it solid. For that would close the underwater doorways to the beaver cabin. And beavers do not hibernate. They go out for food all winter and cannot simply sleep and wait for spring.

The cabin is generally built by the shore of the pond or

swimming a log to the dam

THE SECURE
WINTER CABIN

snow

ice

water

tunnel

tunnel

pantry

dam

shredded
cedar
bed

water
door-
way

combing
claws

ICE

bubble
breathing

on some little island in it. And the submarine doorway leads by an underwater tunnel up through the cabin floor. There are at least two such tunnels and sometimes more, according to the number of beavers living in the house. The tunnels are fourteen inches wide or so, but for two big beavers to pass in one is not convenient. And as the family grows, if six or seven beavers all wish to leave the cabin at once, because of some danger, the more exits the better. Inside the cabin is a dome-shaped room about seven or eight feet across, with a ceiling perhaps three feet above the floor. The floor is only a few inches above the water so that a beaver cabin is not as dry a nesting place as a woodchuck's den. But they are water squirrels and do not mind the damp.

They keep warm; for the cabin, made very roughly like an upturned bowl, has walls of logs, branches, and mud three feet thick or so. A few cracks are left in the top for air, and on cold winter days you can tel' when the beavers are at home by the warm vapor rising like smoke from an old Chippewa bark tepee. Though very rough outside, the inner walls of the cabin are quite even. Wherever a branch sticks through the mud during building, the beavers simply cut it cleanly off with their big, sharp, orange chisels.

The big room is partly bed and partly dining and drying room. The floor is a little higher where the beavers make their beds of shredded cedar wood. Grass is bad bedding for beavers for it gets soaked when they bring it through the underwater tunnels. But a big chip, chiseled out of a cedar tree, can be brought in and only its outer surface will be wet. This dries soon and it can be shredded into a fairly soft, dry bedding material. When beavers come up into the cabin through the water tunnel, they drip in the dining room before climbing onto their beds. If not sleepy, they comb their hair with special split toenails on the second toe of each hind foot which you can see in the drawing.

They do a great deal of going out and coming wetly in. For no food is stored indoors. It is all beneath the ice deep in the pond, stuck in the bottom mud. In the fall they cut many live branches and put them there, under water, beside the cabin. To get these branches they cut trees not more than eighteen inches thick as a rule, but they have been known to tackle a great tree four feet thick which takes three or four whole nights of gnawing to bring down. Such a tree supplies food for a whole family for a long time in winter. A hungry beaver dives through the tunnel and, swimming under the ice, goes to this pantry, cuts off a stick, swims back up into the cabin, and, dripping pleasantly, eats off all the bark and twigs. He does not eat the wood of the stick nor leave it to clutter up the floor. Out he goes with it and lets it float down to the dam beneath the ice. Then back he goes indoors. Two trips for one meal. Such a wetness!

Of course, during all this submarine swimming he has

to hold his breath which he can do for five minutes comfortably, and twice as long if he has to. If the ice is not very thick, the beavers try to keep blow holes open where they can come for breathing spells. Sometimes bubbles come floating down the stream just under the ice. These can be breathed. Or if there is no other way, a beaver can breathe out, making a big bubble under the ice. While he holds his breath the air in his bubble is purified in the water and he breathes it in again. Thus he is able to make long swims beneath the ice, always protected by it from the cold and from his hungry enemies. Bobcats, wolves, and wolverines track through the snow across the frozen pond to sniff wistfully, smelling the nice, warm beaver meal inside the cabin. But they cannot enter. The bears are sleeping but even they could not claw the cabin open. Its tangled sticks and mud are frozen solidly and it is very strong.

So winter is a generally peaceful time for beavers. Besides the branches stored, water lily roots and some green things grow in that quiet underwater world beneath the ice. But with spring come dangers. Not only do the streams run very full and strong, straining the dam which must never be allowed to break, but all the old enemies are abroad. The bears awakening from hibernation are savagely hungry. They and the wolverines may come and claw at the thawing cabin walls and sometimes they succeed in tearing it wide open. But beavers often keep a burrow in the bank of their stream to which they flee if this occurs. Here they

Three Big Tough Boys of the Weasel Tribe

Wolverine

Badger

Otter

are more safe from mighty claws, though much less comfortable than in the cabin. The water squirrels even have a water weasel to worry about, a wonderful but bloodthirsty animal called the otter. His food is mostly fishes, but baby beaver is a tidbit too. And he can swim through a beaver tunnel as easily as a land weasel creeps down a ground squirrel's hole.

Four or five baby beavers are born in the cabin some time in May. They weigh about one pound apiece. Their eyes are open, they have fur and look like pudgy little models of their parents, paddle-tails and all. In a few days they enjoy swimming in the water where the tunnel comes up through the cabin floor. But they are two weeks old before they dive down through the tunnel and come out at the surface of the pond for their first peep at the world. With their little eyes just level with the water, the pond must look very wide indeed. They scarcely see the banks, but the tops of the tall trees and the great blue bowl of the sky and the bright warm sun must be exciting to these chisel-tooth water babies.

At first they want to swim ashore and play in the shallows and on the bank, and fall asleep in the cozy sunshine. But their watchful mother is always there. She knows that many enemies are skulking through the woods. Before long the babies, frightened by perhaps a fox or bobcat or a swooping hawk, realize it also. And as they grow a little older they go ashore in daytime less and less. Presently they do not come out at all till dusk. Their day begins at sunset and ends with morning. All the beavers' wonderful works are done in the dimness of night, which makes them all the more remarkable.

While the babies are young, father beavers leave home for spring vacations. Like other squirrel tribe daddies, they aren't exactly welcome around the nursery. Sometimes they leave the pond entirely and go off upstream exploring, often building temporary bank burrow homes. Several may keep "Bachelor Hall" together. But by early summer they are back, giving an eye to everything, patching the dam where it needs it, bringing new mud to fix up the cabin walls, worn by the winter and the rains of spring. The youngsters try to help them and, perhaps by working with the old folks, they learn how things should be done about a beaver colony. The young beavers live with their parents until they are two years old. By that time there are perhaps four younger brothers and sisters in the house and still another brood of babies expected any minute. So when father goes forth on his annual leave, the first four young ones, now full grown, leave with him. They meet and mate with other young beavers and build cabins of their own, and so a colony grows.

How they meet is interesting but first I must explain about musk. Musk is an animal perfume. It is very strong in odor and lasts a long time. Human nostrils do not enjoy it full strength. But for hundreds, perhaps thousands, of years, perfume makers have added a little musk to the sweeter, more delicate flavors of perfume people like. This makes them more powerful and longer lasting without spoiling them. Skunks and civet-cats have scents which are too much of a good thing for people to enjoy, though a least little hint of skunk perfume in the woods is to many people very pleasant.

There are musk-deer, musk-oxen, musk-pigs, muskrats, and numerous other musky animals. And like the muskrats, their cousins the beavers have two little perfume sacs on their undersides from which they can give out this animal perfume when they wish. So beavers who have no mates make perfumed mud valentines which they leave along the shore of the streams and ponds they live by. They scoop up mud and make a pie or patty and put some of their musk perfume upon it. The damp mud keeps the odor fresh and strong, wafting their message on the breeze. And other unmated beavers coming along the stream read these messages which tell them very plainly that their mates may soon be met with close at hand.

Perhaps you have always thought that rodents and other animals walk on their hind legs and carry things like people only in the funny papers or in comic motion pictures. But beavers really do. To repair his cabin a beaver scoops up as much mud from the bottom of the pond as his two arms will hold. He swims to the cabin and walks up its rough and tumble sides on his hind legs till he reaches

the spot where the mud is needed. Here he sets it down
and presses it in place with his hands and nose, never with
his tail as so many people still believe. His tail is not a
trowel. It is not used in mud plastering but only to keep
him from falling backwards when he totes the heavy mud
up out of water, walking like a man.

Though he has no trowel, a beaver does have those other
tools of which he makes so great a use. When he goes to

cut a tree he stands as high as he can. Turning his head sideways he bites out as large a chip as he can chisel. Then he bites out another lower down. And then he bites out the piece left between the first two bites. This is just what a man does with an ax. The first chop high, the second chop low, and the third chop—out comes a chip. Around and around the beaver goes till finally falls the tree. Trees near the pond generally lean a little toward it and fall that way. It is easy then to cut them up and swim them home. But further back from the pond trees fall in every direction, sometimes most unhandily. Sometimes they do not fall at all though cut clean through, but stand there dying, held up by the branches of others. This is something the otherwise clever beavers are not able to do much about. Though squirrels of a sort, they are too heavy to climb high enough to free the tangled boughs and let the cut tree tumble. And so sometimes much wood is wasted.

When all the edible trees are gone from the shores of the pond, the beaver colony must find a way to reach trees further back or move. If the land along the banks lies fairly level, they will dig long canals to distant groups of trees and float the new supply of timber home. If the new trees they need are up a hill, they hunt for a spring of water near them. If they find one they dig a canal down hill to the pond, putting little dams in it every so often. They dig a ditch from the spring to this canal. It fills one dam after another till they have a water stairway down which they

canal
to distant trees

a water-stairway down the hill

can float and drag their new supplies. But eventually they have to seek a new place, build another big dam, and make new cabins.

So sometimes beavers come and set to work where none were ever seen before by anyone now living. For though they are protected now by law, for two hundred years they were trapped so much for their splendid fur that in most of our country and much of Canada they entirely disappeared. Sometimes, protected as they are, they start their dam building and wood cutting in very bad places. Bad, I mean, because it makes such trouble for certain people. These people must get permission to catch the beavers alive and move them to some place where they will do no harm.

Beavers may try to dam up railroad culverts. They do not understand about our railroads. Then their pond raises the water up to the tracks and makes the earth so soft that rails spread and trains are wrecked. Or they may flood a farmer's fields and cut down his orchards.

Often their dams do good, for they save up water in the streams when the weather is dry too long. They keep the spring rains from rushing down the streams too fast.

Where a colony has lived a long time and finally moved away, the dam slowly falls to pieces and the pond disappears, leaving only the original stream. But where once had been a forest of trees, most of which were not the kinds men need at all, a fine rich meadow has been cleared. Settlers move in and feed their cows and horses on land they never had to cut a tree upon, nor blast a stump with dynamite. The beavers did the whole job for them.

And they are so very interesting. When they are not harmed by mankind they become very tame and at dusk people can have the pleasure of watching them at work. Baby beavers have been brought up on evaporated milk, nursing from regular baby bottles when they have lost their mothers. In olden times an Indian, trapping parent beavers for their furs, brought a baby beaver home if there was a very young papoose in his tepee. The Indian mother nursed the little beaver just as she did her own baby, raising the child and its pet together. Many Indians believed that their own ancestors were beavers and that the world had been built by giant beavers a very long time ago. And there *were* giant beavers in America a very long time ago, for that matter, whose heads were only four inches shorter than a lion's!

Beaver fur was used as money when the first white people settled in America and for a long time afterward. It long had been used in trade as money by the Indians. And it was the one product of the great American wilderness that the merchants back in Europe wanted and would pay for. The furs were bought by the people of Europe and by the makers of felt beaver hats, once very stylish. At first the white men only traded knives, guns, kettles, etc., with the Indians for the fur. But the value of the fur became so great that finally Dutch, English, and French settlers went trapping in the wilderness themselves, always going further and further westward. Trading posts grew up to which many Indians also brought in furs. There were fights and feuds and trappers' wars amongst the different nationalities of white trappers over who had a right to take the beavers from the streams. The fighting ended many years ago, but the trapping went on year after year until the poor beavers were all but done for. Then, not so many years ago, good laws were made to save them.

In many places beavers had given up trying to live in comfortable cabins and only dug refuge burrows in stream banks. There are some beavers left in Europe and northern Asia, but they all gave up cabin building long ago, for they have been hunted ever so much longer than our own. But at last here in America, in many parts of the United States and Canada, we are getting more and better chances to see these wonderful water squirrels and their wondrous works.

MOUNTAIN-"BEAVER"

A CHISEL-TOOTHER WITH NO NEAR RELATIVES ~ (THE NEAR-EST IS THE REAL BEAVER) ~ THIS CHAP LIVES IN WET REGIONS IN SOME OF OUR WESTERN MOUNTAINS ~ HAS MANY LONG, DAMP TUNNELS ~ IS DARK BROWN AND THE SIZE OF A MUSKRAT ~ ALSO CALLED SHE-WAL-LAL BY CHINOOK INDIANS.

8

RAT, MOUSE AND COMPANY

MUSKRATS AND THE MEADOW MOUSE RELATIONS

PLENTY of people think that rats are horrid but mice are cute. Some people shudder and even scream when they see either rats or mice. Although it is foolish to be so disturbed, these people are more correct than those who think that rats and mice are different. The only important difference between a house mouse and a rat in the barn is the size. We could say the mouse is a small kind of rat or the rat is a large kind of mouse. Both belong to Rat, Mouse and Company, a company which includes a very great variety of chisel-tooth rodents.

Many resemble common house mice and rats in the build of their bodies and the way they live. But others live in trees and bushes like the squirrels, and some in burrows like ground squirrels and moles. Some have spines amongst their fur for protection from their enemies, seeming thus to imitate the porcupines. Others have very long hind legs for leaping like kangaroos. Then too, there are several kinds of rats which live near and in the water somewhat as beavers do—muskrats, for example.

Muskrats always seem as though they are just big rats which wish with all their hearts that they were beavers. They seem to try with might and main to be like their water squirrel cousins. They never quite succeed, not having learned tree cutting nor the importance of building dams. But many muskrats build cabins in ponds raised by the beavers' dams. They even go and live with the beavers. Not right in the beaver cabin but in its very thick walls. Here they hollow out a smaller living room of their own, with tunnels which go down and connect under water with the beaver tunnels.

Nobody finds any fault. The beavers and their admiring cousins must meet very often but everything goes along peacefully. The muskrats, swimming under the winter ice, may even help themselves to a stick or so from the beavers' underwater pantry. But they prefer to look for lily roots and stems or dig up fresh water clams. Once in a while they are able to catch carp and other slow fishes, and in summer they eat frogs and salamanders, worms and insects. They go across the fields and help themselves to sweet corn and other vegetables, apples and other fruit. Some farmers think muskrats eat hens' eggs too. But mainly they eat the roots and stems of water plants and only once in a long time do they bother a farmer.

Muskrats live all over North America and of course millions of them have never even seen beavers, much less lived with them. But they do many things as beavers do for all that. They make both kinds of homes—cabins and burrows in the bank with tunnel openings under water. The cabins are made of lighter materials than beavers use, muskrats being so much smaller (about one foot long not counting the tail). No pile of food is stored beside their cabins, for often the cabin is itself the food pile. They heap up cattails and other water plants on the bottom of the pond or stream until the pile stands out of water like a haycock, a roughly rounded mound. Much of it is edible and during the winter they eat a good deal of their living-room walls. But it is said that muskrats are wise enough to have the walls thickest on the north side to turn away the icy winds. The winter sun, when it shines, can toast through the thinner south side and make the muskrats feel right cozy. Cabins are made also with sticks and sod and mud added to the cattail stalks, more truly in the beaver fashion. But if the cabins are built in streams, they are washed away each spring by the rush of the waters and must be rebuilt every autumn. Perhaps that is why the young ones are born and raised in the bank burrows where high water cannot reach them. During flood times the muskrats may wander far and wide seeking good places to make new homes. Sometimes they leave the streams and ponds to travel overland. Though peaceful animals, muskrats are brave. If you meet them so far from water that they cannot reach it quickly, they will charge at a dog or man and try ferociously to fight their enemy.

On the other hand, if you watch quietly near their homes they will get used to you and go about their affairs without a fear. I have had them come up on the stream bank where I sat, shake the water from their fur, and go to cleaning up. You would not think that animals which spend so much time in water would have to clean up at all. But alas, sometimes they have lice which must be done away with. Once I lifted two baby muskrats from their nest in a hollow log which lay out with its underside in the water. They were full of large red lice. The lice don't drown when muskrats swim, because water does not wet through the thick fur. I put them back and hoped their mother would come soon and give them a good going over!

Mother muskrats in the south may have five litters a year of from three to a dozen babies each. Further north three litters is the rule. But even that makes about thirty-six babies a year. No wonder, though trapped everywhere

Muskrat

Sniff
Sniff

Round-tailed Muskrat

Australian
Beaver-rat

WSB

year after year, they have not disappeared as the beavers almost did. Their fur is rich and dense like the beaver's, only shorter. Millions of unlucky muskrats go to market every year because of this. But all is not sold by the furriers as muskrat fur. Often the outer coat of long coarse hair is plucked, leaving only the soft under fur. This is dyed and called Hudson seal or electric seal. Sometimes it is called river mink.

How the poor muskrat would hate it if he knew that his hide had been falsely named after his enemy! For the mink is of the dreaded weasel family which has a great variety of members, seemingly one or more kinds to prey on every near-by kind of rodent.

Pine martens capture tree squirrels. Badgers and weasels go for ground squirrels. Wolverines and otters worry beavers. Otters and minks catch muskrats in the water or their burrows. And to think that muskrat fur is sold as river mink!

Muskrat meat is sold in some large city markets as "marsh rabbit." It tastes all right but many people who eat rabbit would not buy it if they knew it was rat, even muskrat. The musk does not spoil the flavor of the meat. Muskrats are very cleanly creatures and there is no reason why the flesh cannot be used for food. Almost the entire chisel-tooth tribe is fit to eat and is used as food by many other kinds of animals. Besides human hunters and minks, muskrats are hunted on land by coyotes, hawks, and owls, and in the water by large pickerel.

Muskrats are often seen in the daytime but, like beavers, they are generally busiest at night. During the day they like to sleep under the overhanging bank of the stream. At dusk they rouse to work and play and to feed themselves. Sometimes a muskrat plays all by himself, chasing his tail in the water, swimming in circles. They have favorite spots where they take their food to eat it, a rock perhaps which sticks up out of water, or a stump at the water's edge. It is always a place where they can see what is going on and spy approaching enemies in time to dive to safety. When diving they slap the water with their tails. It is the warning signal of the beavers, though not as loud. The muskrat's tail is flattened like an eel's, the opposite way from the beaver's. It serves as a rudder and its width is increased by a ridge of hairs along its top and bottom edges. The hind feet are partly webbed as if in imitation of the beavers. Muskrats also know the beaver bubble-breathing tricks when swimming under ice.

It would be a good thing if the muskrats could learn the proper beaver way of using dams, because they sometimes spoil dams without intending to by burrowing tunnels through them. When the precious water runs away they do not know it is their fault. Dams and dikes and levees built by man are jolly places to tunnel into, so a-tunneling they go. And much as they seem to enjoy living with beavers they innocently, cheerfully, but very foolishly dig in the beaver dams as well. The beavers patiently patch up holes as fast as they find them. One could hardly blame them if they thought their smaller relatives a bit ungrateful. If they did, they might try to teach them better manners. But it is not likely that the beavers even know who is always making so much extra work for them. So the poor cousin muskrats will never fully learn to be like beavers though it seems to be their dearest wish.

A few muskrats were taken to Bohemia some years ago to live in the fish ponds of a wealthy nobleman. They multiplied rapidly and burrowed through the banks of his ponds doing great damage. They spread out into the whole countryside, growing very large on farmers' crops. But the quality of their fur became far less lovely. It so often is unwise to transplant animals this way. Our gray squirrels have made trouble in England and South Africa. English sparrows and starlings are great trouble-makers here. And English rabbits in Australia are a terrible problem as you will see when we reach the rabbit chapter.

Muskrats do not naturally live anywhere but in North America. Yet there are rats in other parts of the world which live in and near the water very much as muskrats do. In Australia, which has few rodents, is one kind called the beaver rat. All its feet are webbed, the hind feet more than the front. It is seen along the banks of rivers and sometimes on the seashore. The fur on its back is blackish brown sprinkled with golden hairs and its undersides are colored like golden straw, as is the tip of its black tail. In Peru, in the high mountain streams, live water rats with hind feet which are not only webbed but have hair fringes on them. This may help them swim still better. They probably need to be very good at it since their food is mostly fishes.

In Florida we have a water rat called the round-tailed muskrat. It is about eight inches long not counting the tail which is not flattened like the tails of real muskrats. There are no webs on its feet though it swims very well, living about the streams and swamps of Florida and Georgia. It spends less of its time in the water than muskrats do and builds no cabins there. But it does build platforms of grass in shallow water. Here it sits to eat the watery plants and roots it most enjoys. There are prairies there which are wet and mucky, where firm land is hard to find. In many wide stretches, where it looks as though a man could walk, there is only a layer of heavy moss floating on mucky water. The round-tailed muskrat builds platforms in these bogs and rounds up a nest of grass and moss. It has a front and back door and just room inside for turning comfortably around. The doorways lead to tunnels in the muck or to runways through the moss and ferns and rushes of the bog.

I wonder if the mouse or rat who lives in swamp or bog enjoys the odors which pervade his home. He often sniffs the air. But is he thinking of some lurking enemy?

Or does he sometimes sniff for sniffing's sake, inhaling the sweetly scented vapors always rising round about him and finding them lovely? For there is no smell in nature more choice (at least to me) than the aroma of marsh grasses which have grown in rich wet ground, ripened in the clear warm sunshine, died and dried, and as they slowly sink are wet again. Then, as through summer days the water lowers with the same sun's rays, the second drying of the grass sends out a fragrance which can never be described. It seasons life and makes the taste of living fine! Do you suppose the swamp rat ever feels that way about it? Does he like and know he likes it?

The English have a water rat which they call a vole. It lives not only in the streams and wetter swales of England, but all through Europe and east as far as China. It is about the size of a common house rat, but has dense, dark reddish, shiny fur which sheds the water like a duck's feathers. It swims very well, although its feet are not webbed. This water rat makes no muskrat-like houses but burrows into the stream bank for a place to make its nest. Still other water-loving chisel-tooth chaps, which we shall come to later, are related more to guinea pigs and porcupines than to rats.

If there were no other rodents in the world except rats and mice, the chisel-tooth tribe of animals would still be very large. When we think of mice we mostly think of house mice. And many of us think that mice are for the most part small animals which live in people's houses. How many people, when picking wild flowers in the fields and meadows, realize that they are wandering in the world of mice? It is here and not in our houses that most mice live. Though millions may live in the walls of buildings, countless billions fill the fields. So many kinds of mice there are, and so many of each kind.

The hawk, at his cruising speed, skims low over the fields. The owl at dusk and all night long will do the same. They are hunting mice and many are their victims. The fox watches till the grass blades move as a mouse pushes about unseen beneath. He rears on his hind legs and pounces on the spot. Then pressing firmly on the grass he parts it with his teeth till he can snatch his supper. Weasels and other members of their tribe can get a living here. Wildcats and country house cats take many trips into this happy hunting ground. So do small terriers and other dogs. Snakes hunt here and many mice go down the gullets of large bullfrogs. If in danger near a meadow stream, mice sometimes dive in and swim like miniature muskrats. But there is danger in the water too. For trout will take a mouse meal when they can. Crows take their toll and even seagulls. In wilder places coyotes, wolves, and bears eat mice.

But in spite of all these enemies the mice are not discouraged. They go on having multitudes of children, many of whom are eaten but many of whom grow quickly up to have still other children and so on. The farmer knows when his fields are full of meadow mice. And they can cost him dearly. For though the mice may eat a few small insects they really live upon his hay-grass and his grain. They get into his garden and in winter, under the snow, they eat the bark from his orchard trees and sometimes kill them. In summer he may drive his mowing machine around the nests of meadow larks and other insect-eating field birds. But he would not think of driving around the mouse nests. He'd have to give up farming if he were so tender-hearted.

The short-tailed chubby meadow mice make miles of winding paths along the meadow floor. You cannot see them without getting down and parting grass and weeds. They are clean and smooth, kept so by the tread of many little feet, and tiny chisel-teeth cut short all plants which try to grow upon them. It makes travel pleasant for the mice. But I am afraid it makes mouse hunting very easy for the snakes. Sooner or later along these paths the snake will come upon a mouse nest either on the ground or down a little burrow. Here he may catch a grown-up mouse. But if not, it is always likely there are babies to be had.

Pine mice, which are much like meadow mice, make their pathways just beneath the surface of the ground, like moles. Every so often a hole is poked up to let in air. This is perhaps a safer kind of runway but it must be much more troublesome to make. Sometimes they connect with the endless underground tunnels of the moles. Moles

Meadow Mouse

Pine Mouse

MOLE ~
BREAST~STROKE
DIRT SWIMMER

"swim" through the earth after angleworms and insects. Pine mice like to run in these ready-made burrows. But they are not pursuing worms and insects, being vegetarians. So they damage crops by eating roots, bulbs, potatoes, and so on, becoming quite a nuisance when they come to live in people's gardens. In winter, like the meadow mice, they gnaw the lower bark of fruit trees. For the most part, though, pine mice burrow in fields near underbrush about the edges of the forest.

In the forest itself are two other kinds of chubby mice, both very prettily colored: the red-backed mice and the rufous tree mice. Red-backed mice eat seeds, berries, and roots and store these away in hollow logs and other dry places or in chambers underground where they also have their nests. In Alaska, although they are very small, they are hunted with bow and arrow by Eskimo boys, and Eskimo girls use their bright red skins to make fur robes for wooden or walrus ivory dolls.

The rufous or red tree mice, living mostly in Canada and our northwest, have longer tails than their relatives of field and forest. But a greater difference is their habit of living in trees sometimes one hundred feet above the ground. Their nests are made of twigs and the ribs of pine and spruce and fir needles. A needle rib is a thin stiff fiber which runs the needle's length right down its middle. It is not eaten but is dropped on top of the nest where the mouse eats its meals. Much needle rubbish is added to the pile each day. For since needles are the only food of red tree mice and contain very little nourishment, a great many must be eaten. The mice therefore cut and carry home each night a pile of twigs containing needles for a whole day's dining. They eat and sleep and nibble and nap all through the day. A mouse may eat as much as its own weight of needles in a day and a night, and the nest grows larger rapidly with the leftover twigs and needle ribs.

Only one mouse lives in a nest. Large nests built near the tree trunks belong to females. Small ones out on the branches belong to males. The large female nests are often built on old deserted squirrel nests. The larger they get the more rooms they may have, with passages between. One room will be used as living room and nursery in which to raise the twins. And one is very likely to be set aside as toilet. Though they build upon old squirrel nests and live in trees, red tree mice are much more cautious climbers than the squirrels are. Their young ones don't even climb out of the nest until they are almost one month old. And grown-ups cannot leap about from tree to tree as squirrels do. And also, unlike squirrels, they store away no food since needles are forever handy. Neither do they hibernate.

In the coldest portions of America and Asia and Europe, away up north, live the meadow mice called lemmings. They are fitted out with heavier coats than other meadow mice and wear fur gloves. That is, the soles of their feet are covered with wool. There are a number of different kinds of lemmings all very much alike in looks and ways of living. But the lemmings of a certain kind in northern Canada do something every winter which no other mouse members of the chisel-tooth tribe can do. They change their brown fur coats for others of pure white, which makes them look like five-inch polar bears. And they make another change. All lemmings have strong fore-claws for digging burrows in the hard and often frozen earth and for tunneling under heavy snow to find the grass and moss and lichens which they eat. But together with the white overcoats, these unusual lemmings order extra digging tools from nature's great supply house. As the white hairs grow and gradually displace the brown, big horny pads form under the two largest claws on their front feet. These probably make digging easier. Just why they need such special fixings would be hard to tell. For other lemmings get along very well without them.

Sometimes they get along very much too well. Once in a while the meadow mice far to the south have swarmed across the countryside as the squirrels also used to do. But their northern relatives, especially the brown Norwegian lemmings, make much more mighty marches. They are famous for it. Every ten or twelve years since very ancient times they have held their big parades. They begin at their homes in the mountains of Norway, and millions move in a great migration. Straight west they go toward the wide Atlantic Ocean. And no matter what they come to on their way they will not be turned back. Hardly can they be turned aside. A mountain with great high peaks is not marched around. They climb it and go down the other side, due west as always. At a swift stream or wide river they do not search along the banks until they find a bridge

Westward Ho! ~ But, oh! ~ ~ ~

or easy place to cross. In they plunge and swim it where they are. In the valleys they march right through the farmers' fields, eating his crops as they go. His haystacks are not marched around. The lemmings eat right through them. If a worried farmer stands in their path they snarl and bite at him, jumping up and nipping at his trousers.

This great migration of short-legged little chisel-toothers may take three years to finish from the mountains to the sea. Young lemmings are born along the way. And they in turn, when only six months old, can bear more young to swell the mighty ranks. It is a very terrible thing for farmers and other people who happen to live across their path. For they ruin crops, eating even the roots of growing plants as well as harvested grain. They swarm in hungry millions through the villages, and they must be worse than the rats of Hamelin Town. For they often drown by scores in the water of brooks that people use for drinking. They fall down wells and die there by dozens.

In olden times these many lemming deaths caused human deaths to follow. People did not know so well how to protect themselves from sickness in those days. They simply said, "We have a plague of lemming fever"; then they continued to drink the water and to die of typhoid. Some people still believe that lemmings once had a homeland in the west to which they are trying to return. This land was supposed to have sunk to the bottom of the sea, but the lemmings are thought still to expect to find it where it ought to be. It is true that on reaching the great Atlantic they do not stop but swim right in, still heading ever westward as though they thought more land could not be far away. And no doubt they do expect to find dry land by swimming west. But they have no idea how wide or deep the water is in which they swim. Just as they did not hesitate to swim the streams and lakes of Norway, they will attempt to swim through any other water in the same way. So, many thousands drown and the grand march ends in Davy Jones's locker.

Some people think that every dozen years or so the poor lemmings all go slightly crazy, that they all suddenly wish to commit suicide by drowning in the Atlantic. But they would not have to go so far. The first water they came to would do as well. No, they move because their food supply at home is very low. Too many lemmings have had too many young ones for too long a time. Too many animals of one kind are living in one place, and from sheer hunger most of them start out to seek their fortunes elsewhere. Just why they will only go straight west nobody knows. But the Pilgrims and the other settlers who sailed westward to America from Europe, and the pioneers who crossed our great wide land to the Pacific, always hoped to better their

Harvest Mice
at home

131

condition further on. And just as many a pioneer never reached his land of promise, so many a lemming dies on the long trek west. Sickness, hunger, treacherous rivers, wild animals, and wild Indians killed many people westward bound. Sickness, hunger, treacherous rivers, lakes and the sea, and wild animals kill off millions of lemmings as they go. Hawks, owls, wildcats, and weasels follow them, eating from this walking pantry day and night till the march is ended. In Norway animal enemies of rodents are not as many as in America, and so the lemming marches are oftentimes tremendous. Always a few are left behind and they live comfortably on what food is to be had. When the mighty hosts have gone, the plants have a chance to grow in plenty once again. Young lemmings soon are raising healthy families which soon are raising others. And in ten years after the last great march there will be millions more to march again.

9

RAT, MOUSE AND COMPANY

LONGER LEGS AND TAILS, BIGGER EARS AND EYES

SO far I have told about the chubby, short-eared, small-eyed, mostly short-tailed members of Rat, Mouse and Company. Muskrats don't have short tails by any means, but they are closer relatives of meadow mice, voles, and lemmings than of the other long-tailed rats and mice. Were we to put in this one book all the things which are known about these other rats and mice, it would be fatter than a great old-fashioned dictionary. We can include but a few of the most interesting.

In many of the same fields with meadow mice may be

found the very tiny harvest mice. Their name will tell you that they share the blame for damage to the farmers' crops. But they do not invade his gardens as a rule nor do such damage as the meadow mice. Sometimes, because their neat round nests are often built above the ground amongst the stalks of grass or grain, they are brought into the farmer's barns and bins with the harvest. Hence the name. The nests may also be right on the ground or up in bushes. An old bird's nest may be adopted and fixed up to suit their mouse ideas. When climbing they can hold on with their tails like opossums or like American monkeys. Harvest mice live in much of the United States and in all countries to the south as far as northern South America. There are other harvest mice in England, Europe, and Siberia. All are tiny. It takes at least a half dozen of them all together to weigh one ounce! They look like very small common house mice but browner and not so gray.

In our southern states live cotton rats and rice rats which also help themselves to things the farmer raises. The rice rats like to live in rice fields not only for the grain they find there, but because such fields are always wet and often flooded. They live in many boggy, swampy regions. And when muskrats live there too, the rice rats are likely to share the muskrat houses just as muskrats sometimes live with beavers.

In North America and parts of Central America live the wood rats which have two other better names—pack rats and trade rats. The name wood rat is not so good, since though many live in the woods some also live in desert regions. Pack rat and trade rat suit them better. For wherever they live they pack or carry almost anything they can move. Often this is done when building nests. But often it is done apparently for fun. While taking various sticks and stones from one place, they are likely to bring back other small loose objects in their place, trading so it would seem.

Ranchmen or hunters living in the woods are frequently annoyed by their busy tricks. The rats come in while the men are sleeping and carry off most anything they can tote—knives, forks and spoons, tobacco pipes, cartridges, pieces of rope, handkerchiefs, even the shoes of the sleepers. And in their place they bring into the house all manner of sticks and stones and rubbish. When anything is missing from homes where trade rats come, it can probably be discovered in the trade rats' nests.

Trade rats look somewhat like the common house rats which plague people in towns and cities, but their fur is softer and heavier and their tails are not naked and scaly, but covered with hair. In the mountains of California there is a kind of trade rat whose tail is quite as bushy as many a squirrel's. But it trails along behind him as any other rat's tail does, and is not held up high or over his back like a chipmunk's or squirrel's. He runs like a rat and does not go in the short quick bounds of a squirrel. After all he is a rat for all his squirrel-style clothes. He has the musky odor of his muskrat relatives also.

We know that many other rodents store up food and have collecting, saving habits. But with the trade rats the habit is so strong that they collect a mass of things which are sometimes of no use to them at all. Their nests are often several feet in height, a mighty heap of objects piled against a tree or cactus trunk. Some trade rats are better collectors than others. And rats of other breeds will save up things they cannot use. I used to have a large white rat who would take any bright-looking thing I gave him and hide it in his shredded paper nest. It was funny to see him

BLACK RAT

BROWN RAT

sniff a shiny bolt or nut or washer, then take it and excitedly open the side of his nest like a squirrel digging a hole, put it in, and cover it quickly. I don't believe he ever thought of it again, but he enjoyed getting each new treasure.

I don't know what kind of rat family he belonged to. He was an albino of the black rats or Norway brown rats. These two kinds, with the common house mice, are the greatest wanderers of all the chisel-tooth tribe. Many hundreds of years ago the black rats started to wander out of Asia, and they went all over the world, running overland through Europe and stealing rides on ships across the seas. This was bound to happen, for besides getting a living from the garbage and rubbish of human homes they found great stores of food on the waterfronts in warehouses waiting to be shipped abroad. Of course, the rats did not hanker for a cruise or to go and settle in a far country. But sometimes they were rummaging in crates and bags and boxes when these were put aboard the ships. And ships have to be tied to docks by heavy ropes. Over these ropes rats also ran on rummaging trips at night. So many ships cast off their ropes and sailed with extra passengers who had no tickets. When they tied up to other docks in countries far away, the stowaways ran ashore over the ropes again, and there they were.

They never thought "So this is London" or New York or Honolulu, or so on, but they moved right in and set up rat-housekeeping wherever they had landed. They made nests in walls, attics, cellars, sewers, rubbish dumps, wherever they could be concealed, and raised a lot of children. Soon some of these also went to sea till finally there were black rats in every land. Following them much later out of Asia came house mice and the big brown so-called Norway rats. These brown rats were not as sleek and graceful as the black rats. But they were heavier and tougher and wherever they went they drove the black rats out. They could not do much about the mice, for their little relatives could hide in holes too small for big, brown Norway rats to follow.

The name of Norway rat was given them by the English, who thought they landed in England from Norwegian ships. They reached our shores about the beginning of the Revolution. Many people believed they landed from the ships which brought the hated Hessian soldiers. But no one could prove it and the rats probably came on ships of all kinds. The black rats were already here. So were the roof rats. Roof rats are a variety of black rat; they have white bellies. They do not live in America farther north than North Carolina. It is thought they may have come with the early Spanish explorers, perhaps even on the *Pinta*, the *Nina*, and the *Santa Maria* of Columbus.

Possibly the black rats which reached Europe first were already in the Holy Land, the Near East, when armies of the European nations went there fighting in the Crusades.

Mongoose

The rats could easily have come back with them. Or maybe they came even earlier when the terrible Huns, vast armies of wild Mongolians, invaded Europe from the east. Nobody knows. Whenever and however they arrived, they brought much trouble with them.

The rats and mice did not stay on the waterfronts and in the cities. Spreading all through every land they became expensive pests on farms. Today, living in the fields and barns of farmers, they destroy millions of dollars' worth of food and grain each year. They suck hens' eggs and kill young chickens, ducks, and turkeys, just as weasels do. They have been known to kill young pigs and lambs. On large islands in the tropics like Haiti, Jamaica, and Hawaii, they spoiled so much sugar cane that mongooses had to be brought from India to kill them off. The mongooses didn't quite succeed in Hawaii. Some of the clever rats went to living up in palm trees where their enemy cannot go. But at least the sugar fields were saved.

Nowadays we call anyone who takes a share of what we

have, without being invited to, a chiseler. Rats, the chisel-tooth rodents, are the greatest chiselers we know. They may be dangerous gangsters too. In the sewers of great cities they sometimes live by the thousands. And being big and wild and hungry, they may attack the men who sometimes have to work down in the sewers. A man is no match for a thousand hungry rats. He must climb out quickly till something can be done about them.

Because many rats live in such filthy places they have spread much sickness amongst the people whose food they steal. There is a flea which lives on the rats. This flea sometimes carries in its mouth a terrible disease called bubonic plague. If a rat flea of this kind bites a man, he may die of the plague and his sickness spreads to other people. It has killed two million people in one year in India. In olden times before doctors knew how to fight against such sickness, plagues killed millions of people in Europe too. Once it was believed that a dish of fried mice and a bowl of owl soup was the very best cure for whooping cough! How things have changed, thank goodness! Nowadays the scientists and doctors know a great deal more about these things, and are also very watchful. So the danger is not as great as once it was.

There is no danger in keeping the albino rats and mice we see in pet shops. Neither they, nor their ancestors, have lived in filthy places. They are very useful to the doctors, who find out many things to help human beings keep well by making tests on white rats and mice. I know a scientist who had an old white rat named Horace, which had no cage but ran free in his study. Oftentimes at the end of a hard day my friend would be so tired and so busy thinking he would forget to cover the inkwell. Next morning

A MESSAGE FROM HORACE

he would find the ink all gone. The finger prints of the thief would be all over his papers. Sure enough; one look at Horace would show his white toes and whiskers stained blue-black. He drank it every time the well was left uncovered, and later learned to lift the cover off himself. Such liquor would kill most creatures. But not Horace. He died of old age at three and a half years. Some time before his death he became very deaf, but more in one ear than the other. So when you called him he would run in circles, somewhat as do the Japanese waltzing mice. Japanese waltzing mice are black and white or gray and white and very, very nervous. They seem to tremble all the time, even when asleep. When awake they run in circles and figure eights as though madly chasing their tails, or round and round their food dishes. They also dance in couples and by threes, whirling about each other so fast that they blur together before your eyes. All are very deaf but there

Waltzing
Mice

must be something else quite wrong inside their heads which makes them spin that way. They could not live outside of cages where a mouse must be always well to keep alive.

Their ancestors were ordinary Chinese house mice. From these, just as they bred all manner of strange goldfish from common carp, the Chinese probably bred these whirling mice hundreds of years ago. Some were taken to Japan. And long after, such mice were brought from there to America. As we have seen in the case of Horace, when there is trouble with their hearing rats and mice may get a whirling habit. Some ancient Chinese breeder of pet mice must have had two deaf ones which whirled, at least a little. He mated them and their deaf children tended to whirl still more. Gradually, by mating only the whirlingest together, he began this race of mice which always whirl.

The waltzing mice are smaller and weaker than ordinary mice. Nevertheless they are the marathon dancers, the whirling dervishes, of the mouse world. Even babies which cannot yet stand mill around each other in the nest. One must never give the mother cotton to line her nest, for both she and her young are bound to twist in it, winding it round and round until they choke themselves. Sawdust is the safest stuff. Let them run in circles as circus animals do around the sawdust ring.

If I had to be a mouse, I'd certainly choose to be a plain but healthy house mouse. However much some people may dislike them, all must admire their ability to take care of themselves. Not only do they live in spite of endless enemies by having big and frequent families, but many of them are very clever, even learning how to spring our traps and eat the bait unharmed. And many mice are musical. When I was a boy a little mouse would come from a crack in the bricks of our fireplace and appear to listen as my father played the piano. Some mice build nests right in pianos. And many sing. Their notes are not as loud and clear as those canaries make, but they have long trills and chirps which seem to satisfy them very well. A little mouse standing on his hind feet to sing is a pleasant sight and a cheerful sound.

As we have said, perhaps more kinds of chisel-toothers sing in their own fashions than anybody realizes. Not only house mice sing but other kinds as well. In country houses the place of the house mouse may be taken by a larger and more beautiful kind of mouse which also sings. It is known as wood mouse, deer mouse, or white-footed mouse. Wood mouse refers to its usual home in the woods. The other two names refer to its appearance. Like the deer, its eyes are large and liquid-looking. Its ears are big and sensitive. And its fur is a beautiful red-brown color like a deer. On its undersides and feet the fur is white as snow. Its song is a long soft trill, not as high nor as clear as a canary's. It sounds a lot like a woodpecker drilling on a hollow tree far off in the forest.

Deer mice are just as clever as ordinary house mice. They too may find a way to take bait from a trap in safety. It is surprising that any mouse can learn to spring a trap. One would expect a mouse to be too frightened. The sound is so startling. When a trap you have baited suddenly snaps as you put it on the floor, it makes you jump even though you are used to the sound. Think how much more shocking the snap of the trap must be to the tiny, nervous, jumpy little mouse. Yet he can control his fears and find a way to get the bait unharmed. His delicate ears are generally awfully near the trap the first time he hears one snap. Of course he rarely hears it at all if it catches him. But sometimes he does.

I once caught a deer mouse in a trap by the tip of his tail. This I only found out later. All winter a great many deer mice kept coming from the forest into our cellar. I

had to set four traps and caught four mice each night. One morning I could only find three traps. The other had disappeared entirely. After that, though there were still many mice, my traps were always empty. Each morning they would all be sprung and harmless, with the bait gone. They were never where I set them the night before. Some mouse kept pushing them about till they knocked against something and were sprung. I tried fastening them to a board on the floor with nails and tiny wires. It didn't work. The wise mouse simply pushed them as far as the wires would go. This was nearly always enough to spring them and make them safe for eating bait.

But one night a trap must have failed to snap when he pushed it on its wire. He must have thought that it was safe after a good pushing. For I found him next morning where he had died without even knowing anything about it. At the tip of his tail was a purple knob where the missing trap had snapped him months before. I found it behind the screens when springtime came. It seemed a shame to have had to kill so smart a mouse. After all it took good brains to learn even as much as he did about traps. He had never studied about machinery. Yet he learned how to handle it, for a while. The only thing he might have known about before he came into our cellar that was the least bit like a trap would be the jaws of some enemy, a fox, for instance. But after a fox had snapped at him he would hardly go up and tickle its jaws to make it snap again. Yet he knew that tickling a trap till it snapped would make it safe.

Even people who understand machines make mistakes in handling them sometimes. The mouse may have gotten careless or forgotten for one fatal moment. But for over two months he tickled my traps and feasted nightly all because being first caught by the tail had taught him that, once sprung, a trap was no longer dangerous. Not long ago there were photographs taken of a mouse which sprung a trap by pushing an empty matchbox against the spring, then ate the bait in peace and washed up sitting on the trap.

Some of the deer mice moved right in to stay that winter. They made nests in the preserve closet and other places, nests of newspaper lined with wool felt wrapping torn from the water pipes. There was little of our food they could get into but they brought in their own from out of doors. This was mainly a supply of beechnuts which they stowed in great numbers in anything that would hold them, including my rubber boots.

In the spring when cleaning out the cellar I made a rubbish bonfire. Into this I tossed what I thought to be an empty mouse nest. A mother mouse jumped out with three blind, naked babies clinging to her. She was bewildered by the smoke and I caught her by the tail. I put her temporarily into a mason jar with the babies and made a cage in which I put a wooden chalk box with a little hole in one end. I put strips of soft wool cloth and newspaper in the cage, fixed a water dish and food dish full of bird seed and raisins. Then I put the unhappy little family into the cage, went out of the room, and peeked. At first the mother ran about the cage seeking a way out. But soon, seeming to realize there was none and finding good bedding handy, she set to work, carrying it into the box while the babies crawled about the cage floor. As soon as she had made the bed she picked up each crying (squeaking) infant in her chisel-teeth and carried it in. I marveled that the sharp chisel-teeth didn't cut their tender little skins.

But they grew and one day with eyes wide open they came timidly out of the box. At the least sound they would rush back, all trying to go through the hole at once. Soon they were out again, going a little further each time. Presently they were all about the cage playing tag, pick-a-back, king of the castle, and catch mother's tail, as well as jump off the dishes and let's turn somersaults. Their large heads made them look very funny. Their fur was a house-mouse-gray at first but gradually it turned brown and white as they grew bigger and better proportioned. I gave them a tiny tree to climb and a trapeze made of a mutton bone. This was good for trying their new teeth too. Out in the forest where most deer mice live they gnaw the bones of dead animals and the antlers dropped by deer. They add insects to their fare of seeds and nuts and berries. Of course most deer mice do not enter people's houses. They make their nests and store their food in a great variety of places. Some use crevices in rocks or hollow out rooms under logs lying in the forest. Or they find a hollow stump or an empty woodchuck hole. They sometimes use old birds' nests. Being very good climbers they go aloft to hunt for nuts as squirrels do. If they find a handy hollow high above the ground they are likely to build a nest in it and live a squirrel's life, playing tag in the trees and storing nuts and berries in chambers they may find or burrow out themselves. They do not hibernate. Even though you rarely see them in the daytime you find their foot and tail prints everywhere in the snow on a winter morning.

The deer mice belong to a mouse family which is enormous. There are mice much like them living all over North and South America, from the coldest to the hottest places, from the lowest plains to the very high mountains, in damp rich forests and in dry desert places. Wherever they live they store supplies of whatever kinds of seeds, berries, and nuts grow there. They raise several families a year and if they would stay out of our houses we could admire them for the same reasons we approve of chipmunks and squirrels. They are full of energy and work hard. The babies which grew up in my cage would stop playing, when still very small, and toddle into the box with fresh nesting material, helping mother to keep house.

At least one kind of mouse is a real help to the farmer. It is the grasshopper mouse of the United States. It gets its name from its summer habit of eating grasshoppers. Grasshopper mice eat almost nothing else but insects when they can be found, though in winter they fall back on a seed and berry diet since they do not hibernate. In our northern prairie states grasshoppers sometimes grow in such numbers that their flying swarms form dark clouds as they move to settle on fresh fields. Their wings make a roar in the sky like the propellers of a hundred million enemy airplanes invading the land. Small though they are, in such multitudes they bring suffering and destruction with them, devouring every bit of green that grows, ruining crops. This does not happen every summer. But it would happen often were it not for mice which live upon them. The grasshopper mouse springs upon a grasshopper, grasps its shoulders, and bites off its head. Often the hopper is as long as the mouse and its strong kicking legs sometimes tip the mouse over backwards. But the mouse hangs on and soon the legs are eaten along with the rest of the insect. Many other insects are eaten also. In our southwestern states this kind of mouse is called scorpion mouse because he kills so many of the poisonous creatures. He first bites the tail so that the scorpion cannot sting, and then starts eating the head.

This hunting mouse is really very bloodthirsty. He helps the farmers still more by killing and eating other kinds of mice. These he also attacks head first, biting into their brains. He has a fierce look in his face, and he makes short

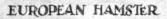

EUROPEAN HAMSTER

This stumpy-tailed relative of our deer mice has cheek pouches, stores food in its burrows, sleeps through coldest weather, has many children, & pesters farmers.

Grasshopper Mouse

squeaks like tiny barking as he attacks his prey. Like a wolf he follows the trail of his enemy, sniffing along the ground. He lifts up his wee head and howls his hunting call. The howl is high and thin because his throat is small but it is mouse howling just the same. When he gets close to his victim, his tail wags like the tail of an excited hunting dog. Then he pounces on his luckless relative. He is indeed a cannibal of the chisel-tooth tribe, a tough, terrible, and terrific mouse. But he is the farmer's friend.

From such wolf-like mice we go to mice which are like kangaroos. There are a number of kinds of kangaroo mice or kangaroo rats, as they are often called. Some are very small, but the largest measures over a foot long counting its very long tail. The longness of the tail helps its balance while leaping over the ground with great bounds of its very long and strong hind legs. Also, as with a kangaroo, its fore-legs are very small. They are used for holding food and for digging burrows and when the animal is moving about very slowly. Otherwise only the big hind legs are used. The little front ones are held so tightly to the breast that there appear to be none there at all.

Kangaroo rats fight as kangaroos do, dancing before each other like roosters, watching a chance, then leaping above their rival and kicking down with their great hind legs. The kick makes a loud thud, sends the kicked one sprawling, and must hurt a good deal. They do not use their teeth in fighting and will not bite when picked up in

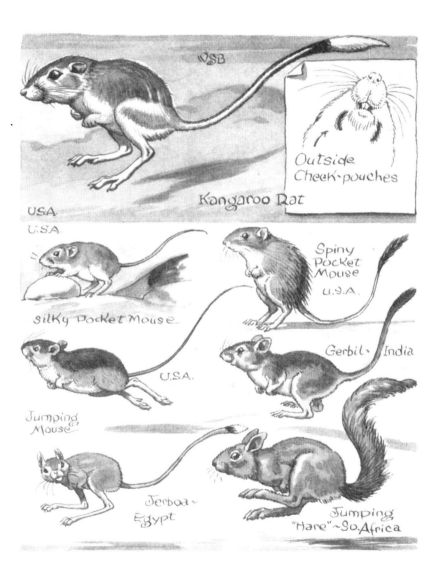

VSB

Outside
Cheek-pouches

Kangaroo Rat

USA

U.S.A.

Silky Pocket Mouse

Spiny
Pocket
Mouse
U.S.A.

Gerbil~India

U.S.A.

Jumping
Mouse

Jerboa~
Egypt

Jumping
"Hare"~So.Africa

the hand. These chaps live in the drier parts of our country where they make their burrows under bushes or cactus plants. The burrows look as though they belonged to much larger rodents. Kangaroo rats cannot creep through holes just a wee bit wider than their bodies like ordinary rats. The tunnels have to be high to accommodate the little fellows' great hind legs. At night they come forth and bound along little roads their feet have worn in many trips to feeding places. They gather and store away great quantities of seeds underground, for they stay awake in winter. The provisions are carried in cheek pouches. But, unlike the chipmunks, their cheek pockets open outside of the mouth instead of inside, and are lined with short fur. Sometimes they store their food and live in old prairie dog holes. And like the prairie dogs they do not need any water to drink. Unlike desert rabbits they do not even eat the juicy parts of cactus to be refreshed. Their digestion turns some of the starch and sugar of the dry seeds they eat into water, and this satisfies them.

Though they sometimes live in old prairie dog holes, their own diggings are visited by uninvited guests. Kangaroo mice and rats stop up their doorways with loose dirt when the night is over. It keeps out the heat of the day. But during the time the holes are open scorpions and cockroaches do crawl in. So do lizards. And sometimes a frightened ground squirrel or cottontail rabbit will dash in for safety from a coyote or hawk. Grasshopper mice come in also for no good reason, as do rattlesnakes. Badgers dig open the winding burrows. Foxes, coyotes, bobcats, and owls wait outside for a meal of kangaroo rat and try to catch them as they work far from the burrow. Out there in the open it pays to have long leaping legs, however unhandy they may be inside the burrows.

In the same regions where kangaroo rats live may be found their little relatives, the silky and spiny pocket mice. They also have long hind legs for jumping and outside cheek pockets for food collecting. The silky ones have the smoothest of shiny fur. The spiny ones have long coarse bristles growing amidst the fur on their backs. But the bristles are not hard enough to save them from their hungry enemies as a porcupine's spines do. Both silky and spiny pocket mice are hunted by the same animals which prey on kangaroo rats.

In Asia and Africa there are other kangaroo-like mice and rats not close relations of our own. But they look and live like them, in dry desert places. They are called jerboas and gerbilles. The largest, which looks least like our kangaroo rats, lives in South Africa. It is called a spring hare or a jumping hare, and it appears to have the head and body of a rabbit, the tail of a squirrel, and a kangaroo's legs. Other smaller kinds look more like our kangaroo rats. The burrows of our kangaroo rats look as though many lived together, there are so many doorways in one mound. But only one lives in a mound except where a female is raising her babies. On the other hand, Old World jerboas get together in colonies and live a very social life. So it is easy for the native people to catch enough to cook for supper in a short time. They close all but one of the doorways of a colony, pour much water into the tunnels, and catch the frightened jerboas as they bound out of the only open door. If they get safely away it is no use to try to catch them. The swiftest hound cannot keep up with their mighty leaping. One of the gerbilles in India, called antelope rat, will suddenly jump back right over a pursuing dog. Before the dog can stop and turn around the jumping chisel-toother is far away and going like the wind.

We have in North America one close relative of Old World jerboas. This is the jumping mouse. It doesn't live in hot desert places like kangaroo mice and rats. But it likes brushy places on the edges of forests and may be seen in mountain regions of California and New Mexico, in the Middle West, New England, Canada, and Alaska. Like the kangaroo rats it has to have a very long tail to keep its balance while jumping. A three-inch animal jumping ten feet is like a man jumping two hundred feet. We should need a balancer too if we could do that. A jumping mouse which has lost its tail turns somersaults in mid air and has a bad time fleeing its enemies. This mouse has cheek pockets and stores food. It hibernates rolled up in a warm nest underground, its nose on its stomach, one great leg on each side of the head, the tail curving up over the head and down the back.

The next chisel-toother is a miner and uses his chisels as pickaxes underground. Here he spends almost every minute of his life. Because of this, his body has a build almost the opposite from kangaroo rats. One thing is the same: he has outside cheek pockets and is called the pocket gopher. But instead of being light and swift of movement, he is thickly built and slow. His weight, instead of being in his hips and hind legs, is up in his neck and head and shoulders. His hind legs are smaller than his front and his tail is short and wears no tuft. But he uses it to feel his way when going backwards as he sometimes does in his many twisting tunnels.

The pocket gopher lives much like a mole. But the mole is only seeking worms and insects, whereas the gopher is after our vegetables and the roots of many plants. He is a very great nuisance in many parts of North America. In Florida a certain type of tortoise which burrows is called gopher. In other places ground squirrels are called gophers. But only the pocket gopher is a real gopher. In the South some people call him salamander, though of course that is not correct. You might as well call a squirrel a toad. Perhaps they simply wish to call him a bad name, and no wonder. He spoils the Georgia sweet potatoes and kills the orange trees in Florida. But whatever people call real gophers, they find them very hard to get along with.

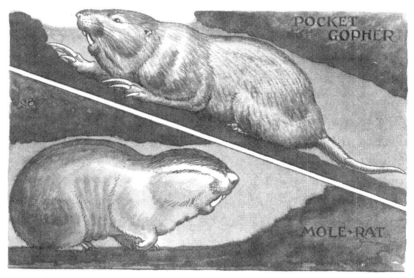

Where a gopher works, one sees a series of dirt piles each with a hole where he has tunneled up to let in air and take out earth. Like those of ground squirrels and prairie dogs, his tunnelings endanger the legs of cows and horses. He digs with his heavy fore-claws and his chisel-teeth which are much longer than his lips. When he has loosened enough dirt, he scrapes it past him, turns around, and pushes it along and out of the tunnel with his forehead and fore-paws.

For ordinary getting about he has to fold his big claws in and plods along as though walking on his knuckles. When he wants to empty his pockets he places a fore-paw behind each one and pushes forward. All the stuff he has collected falls out in the storage chamber: somebody's potatoes, carrots, beets, the roots of fruit trees. He is a grumpy fellow and will fight any other gopher who enters his private tunnelings. Only at night will he come outside, and very little even then. His eyes and ears have shrunk from staying in the dark and underground so much. He does not hibernate.

Similar to gophers are the mole-rats of the Old World. They live and work almost continually underground just as the gophers do. One kind which lives in countries that bound the eastern half of the Mediterranean Sea is entirely blind and its ears are like little warts. Its grayish yellow fur will lie backward or forward with equal comfort as the animal shuttles back and forth in its dark tunnel.

Down in South Africa there lives another kind of mole-rat which can see a little. He is about a foot long but his eyeballs are only one-tenth of an inch in size. His digging claws are very large, as are his chisel-teeth which he does not hesitate to use on other mole-rats which enter his tunnels, or on anyone who tries to take hold of him. He is a good growler and snarler and snaps great hunks out of the air if you come too close, hoping to get a bite at you. He pilfers gardens and steals potatoes. From these he bites all the eyes so that they will not sprout and may be saved for future use.

Living in the sandy soil of Somaliland, East Africa, are the naked sand rats. They are only mouse size, but on their entire loose-skinned bodies are only a few scattered colorless hairs, except for hair fringes on their feet and some scanty whiskers. They have very projecting teeth, no outside ears, and nearly useless eyes. When caught they do not try to bite but give a few soft coughs as though displeased at being taken from their deep studies underground. During their digging, with a stout heave from below they push up little conical mounds of sand which look for all the world like miniature volcanoes.

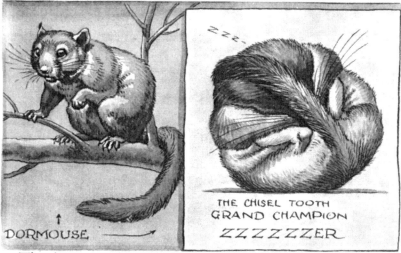

DORMOUSE

THE CHISEL TOOTH
GRAND CHAMPION
ZZZZZZER

The last member of Rat, Mouse and Company is the dormouse. He doesn't take the place of a doorman in the mouse world. Doormen must be always wide awake. The dormouse is far from being so a great deal of the time. You remember the dormouse in *Alice in Wonderland*, who couldn't stay awake and missed about everything which was going on. Every dormouse misses at least half of what happens during its life, for they all sleep six months of every year. *Dorm* means slumber, so a dormouse is a sleep-mouse—perhaps the champion hibernator of all the chisel-tooth tribe. But like the squirrel he is surprisingly lively when he is not dormant.

In fact, he looks like a very small squirrel and has some very similar habits, as our own deer mice also do. Though he sleeps so much, he stores provisions of seeds, berries, and nuts in convenient crannies near the nest. For though he eats very little in the winter, perhaps only waking for a nibble during warm spells, he needs pantry supplies in spring before fresh eatables have grown. The nests are built in bushes or low trees where, in summertime, the mice romp in the branches as freely as squirrels.

Dormice live in England and Europe, where they are often kept as pets, and in South Africa. There are several kinds in Europe. One kind, called the fat or squirrel-tailed dormouse, was raised in cages by the ancient Romans, to be used as especially choice victuals when they feasted. Another kind called garden dormouse is said to be a very busy thief in gardens and orchards, always taking the best and ripest fruits. This may plague the farmer, but it only goes to show that, great sleeper though he is, a dormouse knows his business when he is awake.

The dormice of South Africa build nests in trees but sometimes prefer the grass roofs of Negro homes. They even move into old-fashioned straw beehives and make nests on the top layers of honeycombs. They sleep all day and the bees sleep all night. So there is no trouble. Of course the mice may eat a little honey but they clean up the hive by eating all the dead and dying bees. In fact they are great insect eaters. They eat birds' eggs too, like robber squirrels. When two male dormice fight, the victor eats up the vanquished. But for all this fierce liveliness, they sink into the same long sleep that their relatives in Europe do. For there is a cool season in South Africa, when no dormouse can possibly keep awake.

10

CHINCHILLAS AND OTHER KIN OF PORCUPINES

THE chinchilla is yet another kind of rodent with a squirrelish look, but which belongs in a different division of the chisel-tooth tribe. This division includes with chinchillas an odd assortment of relatives which seem to have no family resemblances. Some are like squirrels and others are more like muskrats, moles, pigs, deer, hedgehogs, and what not. But there are things about their jaws and bones and "innards" which show that they belong together. These are things the scientists must worry about. But here we only need consider the way they look and how they live.

The bushy tail of the chinchilla is about five inches long. The plump body is twice as long and covered with the softest, silkiest, curly, pearly-gray fur. It is an inch thick and so dense that even a flea cannot crawl through to plague its wearer. For this fur chinchillas have been hunted so much in the Andes Mountains, where they live, that they are very scarce. They make burrows and live in colonies in high valleys amongst the mountains where the weather is very cold much of the time, and the thick fur very comforting. But what good is one's fur if hunters come to kill you for it? Let us hope the South American people have made good laws to protect the chinchillas, as we have done to save our beavers. Real live animals are a good deal better than stuffed ones, or pictures of them, or books about them either. Perhaps the chinchillas will be saved by fur farmers. There is one chinchilla fur farm in California, where the animals are being carefully raised from a few wild ones brought here from South America.

South America is the home of almost all the rodents in this chisel-tooth division. Even our North American porcupine's ancestors lived there ages ago as their porcupine relatives do today. And probably the ancestors of Old World porcupines wandered out from there before the continents broke up and drifted far apart, ending all the land connections.

The ancestors of the guinea pigs you see in pet shops came originally from Peru. On the pampas of Argentina live animals which take the place of our prairie dogs. They are called viscachas and are gray with black and white

VISCACHAS

faces. They form colonies of twenty or thirty members, throwing up much dirt about their burrows and clipping all the grass round about as prairie dogs do.

They make one doorway bigger than the rest, with a kind of open cellar vestibule about five feet wide before it. In the banks of this vestibule swallows dig out nesting spots. When the swallows move out other birds called mineras use the nest sites. There is also a burrowing owl like the one which lives in our prairie dog holes. Foxes move in and live with the viscachas and live on the young viscachas too, especially if there are young foxes to be fed. Any viscacha village is likely to have its foxy bogeyman. But some of these towns have lasted for at least a hundred years. So many a viscacha must escape the villain's jaws and grow up to its full length of twenty-two inches and a weight of fifteen pounds. Viscachas try to help each other against such enemies as foxes and weasels. If the farmers and cowboys stop all the holes of a colony to kill the rodents which eat the grain and cattle grass, other viscachas will come from another colony and try to dig them out.

They are very playful and sometimes jump about, whacking the ground with their stout tails. These drumsticks also serve nicely as chairs. Viscachas have playful collecting habits like trade rats. They drag all manner of loose objects to the mounds about their holes. Here the Argentine cowboy goes to look for his lost knife or his revolver, and for sticks of firewood. The viscachas are very sociable amongst themselves and most talkative, perhaps more talkative than any other kind of four-footed animal. They have a great variety of noises, viscacha words, and often talk together all night long. A male viscacha will stop his feeding and utter loud, explosive cries and then go on eating peacefully. It means something in viscacha language even if it doesn't make sense in English. He makes a series of low grunts or a sound like someone clearing his throat. And sometimes he lets out a series of rapid squeals, so piercing that he can be heard about a mile away. If you have chased him into his burrow he can be heard making deep moans down in the earth. But before diving out of sight he will make a sudden note of fear and all other viscachas will repeat it and dive out of sight. If only surprised but not too frightened, the whole colony will sit by their burrows yelling in chorus, suddenly stop, then begin the next verse "singing" ever higher and higher. The bones of their ancestors have been found and they were big as buffaloes! If they also had their yelling parties, it must have sounded loud as thunder.

TUCO-TUCO

Also burrowing in colonies are the tuco-tucos, with gray bodies about one foot long and bright red teeth. They live underground more than viscachas and, mole-like, have small eyes, almost no outside ears, and short tails. Their burrows are very long and winding and very common in South America, especially where the soil is sandy. Tuco-tuco is probably the Indian name. It tries to imitate the sound these animals make. You can hear it all around you coming up from underground when you stand near a colony. It has a metallic ring and seems to be made by the picks of seven times the seven dwarfs, down in there mining emeralds and rubies.

Then there are the coypus which live in the lakes and rivers of much of South America, like muskrats. In Argen-

COYPU

tina they are called nutrias, a Spanish word meaning otters. The fur of coypus is valuable and is sold as nutria on the market, very soft and dense and brownish yellow. They dig tunnels from the water into stream banks as our muskrats do, but they are larger, some old males being two feet long not counting the rat-like tail. They cannot dive as well as beavers, but their hind feet are webbed and they spend much time swimming. In the evening they gather for water frolics and babies swimming with their mother try to get seats upon her back, using her for a water king-of-the-castle game. I dare say the mother enjoys it as much as her eight or nine scrambling water babies.

The Indians of Peru raised guinea pigs for food long before the early Spanish explorers reached their country. Later on Dutch traders came and took some home to Europe, where they were raised as pets. And still later some were brought to what is now the United States. Now you can buy them in most pet stores. There are guinea pig farms where they are raised to sell to scientists who test out ways to cure human illnesses. They are also used as food, though more in South America than in the United States. It is about four hundred years since the Dutchmen took their first pet guinea pigs home and several fancy breeds have been developed in that time. Some have very long beautiful hair, others long hair that stands up in bunches all over their bodies. There are pure white, pink-eyed ones; others are black, brown, cream, or spotted with several colors together.

A great many people believe that guinea pigs have more young ones than almost any other creature. But this is not so. Rabbits and many kinds of rats and mice have larger numbers of descendants. A good mother guinea pig can raise but a few more than a dozen babies a year at the most. She has only two or three in each litter. But as pets they are protected; no hungering enemies catch any of them. They all grow up so their numbers increase very steadily. Of course, it is true that they grow up quickly.

A guinea pig mother may have her first baby when she is only two months old, though she herself is not fully grown.

Guinea pigs are born more grown up than rats and mice. Their eyes are open; they have lots of fur. In a few days they start eating vegetables. In less than three weeks they are completely weaned. They seem to be born so grown up that they never play as most other chisel-tooth babies do. They like to be together all the time but they never romp. Being born almost all grown up doesn't give guinea pigs time to learn very much. Being able to take care of themselves when so young they are, at first, way ahead of helpless baby rats. But by the time the rats finally do grow up, after many months, they are far more wise and intelligent than grown-up guinea pigs. Animals learn best while they are young and growing. The longer it takes them, the more intelligent they are likely to become.

When it is feeding time all the "pigs" on a guinea pig farm start crying loudly and shrilly at the same time, "Quee! quee! quee!" over and over. Quee, spelled Cui, is their name in Argentina. Why this animal was ever named guinea pig is a mystery. It does make slight grunting noises and possibly the namer thought it had a pig-like shape. And probably he was a very poor student of geography and natural history. He seems to have believed that Guinea, which is in Africa, is the same as Guiana, which is in South America. He may have meant guiana pig. But Guiana is one of the ports of South America where no

guinea pigs grow. It all seems very silly. We might better just call them cavies which is what they are, along with their relatives the maras and the mighty capybaras.

The maras, or Patagonian cavies, are about two and one-half feet long and over a foot high at their shoulders. This is because of their straight and rather slender legs which make them look like the little musk deer of central Asia or the mouse-deer of India and Africa. Their tails are very small, their ears large. Though they dig burrows, when frightened they act more like deer, not hiding in the burrows but galloping off to safety over the dry pampas. There are ranches in Patagonia now which raise maras for the meat and fur markets.

The capybaras are the giants of the chisel-tooth tribe, being as large as year-old pigs—that is about four feet long and weighing one hundred pounds! They are also known as water hogs, for, like their little guinea pig relatives, they grunt. They live on the edges of rivers into which they frequently dive and swim, especially if scenting danger. Their worst enemy is the great spotted cat of South America, the jaguar, which hunts along the jungle rivers. Their food is mostly water plants and young tree bark, and they graze in herds of a few to thirty or so. When resting on the river bank, they take turns raising themselves for a look and a listen. At the slightest hint of trouble the whole herd dashes grunting into the stream. Near plantations they are in danger of being shot, for they are too fond of corn, sugar cane, and watermelons.

The other cavy-like rodents are the pacas and agutis, both of which also rush into the water when in danger on the land. There are dangers there as well for such defenseless animals. In many South American rivers are crocodiles and very bloodthirsty fishes. The pacas and agutis are hunted for their flesh by both Indians and white men. The Indians believe that by eating the meat of the swift aguti they will be able to run more rapidly themselves. Pacas and agutis are night animals and stay in their jungle burrows during the day. Agutis are about twenty inches long. Pacas are two feet long and prettily colored with rows of white spots on their very dark brown fur. The hard shells of fallen tropical nuts are easy chiseling for them and they also eat the leaves and roots of many plants.

Again we come to an animal which somehow has reminded its name-giver of a pig. *Porc-épin* is French. It

AGUTI   PACA

means pig-spine, or spiny-pig. Our name porcupine comes from the French name. There are porcupines in South America, North America, Europe, Asia, and Africa. Let us first consider our own North American "porcies."

11

PORCUPINES

IF animals were vegetables, porcupines would be cactus plants. They are certainly the cactuses of the animal world. For they have the same device for protection from anything which might do them harm. A cactus cannot fight and cannot run away. But being covered with such sharp spines, it doesn't need to. And like the very fat man who also cannot fight nor run away, neither can the fat porcupine. He sometimes tries to run from his enemies but cannot keep ahead of any of them.

One of the main differences between animals and plants is that animals move, are animated, while plants must stay wherever they are. The porcupine is a kind of climbing, clawing, gnawing, walking animal cactus, but is safest from his enemies when he acts like the plant, standing still with his spines sticking out in all directions.

There is a word which seems to describe a porcupine moving over the ground even better than it was intended to. It is "plantigrade" and merely means walking on the sole of the foot. A lot of animals walk that way, including people, bears, and many rodents—not like dogs and cats and others which tread only on their toes. Plantigrade has really nothing to do with the idea of moving slowly, for plenty of plantigrade animals run well. But poor old "Porcy" is not only a plantigrade animal. He seems to feel, even when hurrying, that he must not lift one hind foot or one front foot till his other feet are firmly planted on the ground. Just try to run, keeping your left foot entirely on the ground until your right is firmly planted, and so on. You may look animated but you won't go very fast.

Many people believe the porcupine is more animated than he really is. They think he can throw his spines at his enemies. But he cannot do so any more than you can shoot hairs out of your head. However, he can and will stick spines into you if you come too close. You do not have to touch him. Just get close enough for him to strike you with his tail and you will collect a fine assortment of big coarse spines and small ones, needle thin, most painfully in your flesh. They are almost as hard to pull out as fishhooks and for the same reason. Though the barbs are very small there are scores of them on every spine. If not pulled out they work steadily deeper and deeper in. This causes much swelling and great pain, and, in the case of animals who cannot pull the spines out of their noses, it often causes death.

If you are just a little out of reach, a frightened porcupine may back and sidle towards you to within striking distance. We must not blame him. All he asks is to be left strictly alone. He is really afraid when his quills stand up. They are only some of his hairs, changed a good deal, but standing on end in fear. Our own hair does it. The dog's back bristles in fear and fight. So does the cat's and many another animal's. So do a fighting rooster's feathers.

But the porcupine's hair-raising act does not always save his life when certain forest enemies attack. More than one bobcat and puma learns to reach a paw quickly underneath and turn a porcupine over. Once on his back he may be killed and eaten easily. The underside has no protective spines at all. There is a fierce animal of the weasel tribe which knows this. It is called the fisher, a dark, swift, very bloodthirsty creature. If it meets a porcupine walking over deepish snow, it dives into the snow and comes up under the poor fellow. Red stains in the snow show all too well what then becomes of him. Dogs do not fare as well except that they can limp home and have their masters yank out the hundreds of spines which would finally kill them otherwise. Even after that they so hate porcupines that they attack them again and again, going home each time in more misery than the battle was worth.

But porcupines don't go about seeking dogs' noses to use as pin cushions. "Let us alone" is their motto. Even amongst themselves they rarely quarrel. And it is almost impossible for one to fight another. For a porcupine to strike another with his tail would be to fill it with the other's spines unless he hit his rival on the nose, which is not spiny. They never seem to think of biting each other's noses, though their chisels could do much damage if they did. The most they do is push each other back and forth, growling loudly till they think better of it.

They cannot even play with one another as so many other creatures do. No rough and tumble fun for them. Perhaps they make up for it somewhat by their lively conversations. They often travel about in pairs on summer nights, though more may get together. And all night long during their rambles they jabber back and forth. To us it sounds like "Wa-wa-waa-WANK-WANX-eonk-eonk-" etc., in high and low tones. But no doubt they express a great deal to each other that we do not understand.

Pocahontas, my pet porcupine, did a lot of wa-waa talk-

REACH

YAWN

STRETCH

SCRATCH

SCRATCH

POSES
of POCAHONTAS

ZZZ
ZZZ

WSB

ing when I first had her. I would imitate her and she would look at me a moment thoughtfully, and then answer. I do not know what I may have seemed to say, nor exactly what she was saying. But I think she was trying to tell me she was lonesome. For ever since I put a mirror into her cage she has been very quiet.

At first she went and touched her nose to it. Instead of the soft nose of another porcupine, hers touched a hard, smooth something which she could not see. Her spines raised as she backed a little. In a short time she became used to the feel of the looking glass and often pressed her nose and hands against it, trying, I suppose, to go through into that space beyond where the other porcupine always stayed. Now she never smootches the glass, but pauses often as she moves about to gaze intently at her "company."

The only noise she makes now, besides the rustle of her spines and the rasp of her claws as she climbs about, is the grinding of her chisel-teeth. This she does every so often whether awake or sleeping. She crunches them together and makes fast, clacking sounds. And she almost always does it while in search of food. When she finds a luscious tidbit she does make one other sound. It shows her pleasure in the food. She is a mighty smacker. Some day I shall let her go far up in the woods, but for the present she is not having too bad a time. She has things to eat no northern porcupine ever knew about. End slices of pineapple and bananas excite her greatly. She eats them skin and all, sitting up squirrel-like.

Water she will not drink, depending on what she gets from the many kinds of leaves and fruits I give her. She doesn't know how to drink. She tried when I gave her a cup of canned pineapple juice. But she sniffed it up and sneezed and almost choked, and got her nose, mouth, and chin all sopping wet and sticky. And she doesn't know how to lap. Maybe her chisel-teeth are in the way for that. She must be satisfied to eat her drinks. Watermelon is most welcome. She smacks loudly while eating it rind and all. The rind and wet seed clusters of musk melons are appreciated. And she thinks peach parings are delightful. Of course I bring her many leaves to eat, this year's blackberry shoots, new hemlock fronds, wild cherry, birch, and apple leaves. When she picks up a bunch of these she does it exactly like a plump old lady taking up her embroidery. Porcupines are vegetarians. But because wood is a vegetable they have some surprising, often troublesome, tastes. Though they dwell in deep forests, a hunter's cabin or any other house near the woods, with all its furniture, is so much cake and candy as they see it. For years the family of Pocahontas has tried each summer to eat our house.

I believe, next to beavers, porcupines are the greatest rodent wood-cutters, at least in North America. With their great orange chisel-teeth they have carved deep scallops in our porch beams and gouged our little wooden bridges. Not far from here some people went to the city once, forgetting to put the porch furniture indoors. When they returned, not a rocking chair was safe to sit in. Many a woodsman has had his hardwood ax handle chewed to bits. The porcupines probably like the salt left in tool handle wood from the sweat of human hands. Many wild animals hanker for salt. In Minnesota I used to put food into a covered butter tub and hang it in an icy spring to keep it cold. Porcupines would swim in the almost freezing water every night to gnaw the salty wood. The butter would have pleased them too. Probably the cold did not distress them, for porcupines have good fur and are very fat.

It is not usual that tree-climbing animals are of such a heavy build. Bears climb a good deal but nowhere near as much as porcupines. Porcupines sometimes weigh over thirty pounds. But they have very long, strong claws which hook into bark and around branches so firmly that their weight matters little. Pocahontas will swing around a branch on which she is walking and hang by all her claws on its underside like a South American sloth. The tails of her porcupine relatives in South and Central America are long and wrap around branches as handily as the tails of South American monkeys. They act as very useful extra hands.

North American porcupines use their shorter tails in climbing more as extra feet than hands. When backing down a tree trunk the tail feels for the next branch, then

South
American
SLOTH

"I always hang
about this way"

North American
PORCUPINES

South American
PORCUPINE

The tail
is a stout
stool to
sit upon

WSB

rests firmly on it as the feet let go the trunk one at a time to grasp the branch. In going up, the tail reaches sideways and helps lift the heavy body onto a branch above. It is used as a balance amongst the branches also, and as a sturdy stool to sit upon.

In winter porcupines often live in one tree for weeks, not in a comfortable hole like squirrels, but right out in the weather, sleeping in the crotches and living on the bark. After eating the bark from the upper part of one tree they go down and climb the next. Trees frequently die from losing so much bark, but they are all the dining room and bedroom porcupines need for cozy winter living, so fat and furry are they within their spines.

In early spring the female finds herself a den amongst the forest rocks in which to raise her children, which are born in April. Very often but one baby is born, though sometimes there are quadruplets. Some people actually believe porcupine babies are born in eggs from which they hatch immediately. But it is not so and doesn't need to be. For though they have spines amongst their soft, dark brown fur, these are short and soft at first. They harden after being exposed to air for a few hours. Coarse hairs soon appear among them, and the spines and hair grow rapidly for the protection of their young owners. Within two months they are weaned and feeding themselves on leaves, buds, and berries. Then they are likely to wander off into the forest alone to shift for themselves. For like their guinea pig relatives, they are born large and pretty well grown up.

In some places where the forests reach for many, many miles, it is against the law to hunt porcupines. This is because a lost person with no gun to shoot game to eat can easily kill the first porcupine he finds with nothing more than a stout stick. The meat will keep a person alive till he finds his way. It is not the most choice food in the forest, but it is edible. Many a woodsman has eaten porcupine meat and it has kept many an Indian from starving in winter when other game was hard to find. Indians pull out all the spines and use them to make decorations on belts, moccasins, leggings and birch bark baskets and canoes. The sharp ends are sewn between double layers of leather or bark so that only the smooth quills show in the pattern. These are sometimes colored with vegetable dyes. The black-furred skins, minus their spines, may be sewn together when enough have been collected, to make a robe. Fur traders used to buy such skins and sell them as "spring beaver."

There are porcupines of one kind or another in many parts of the world. The European kind looks a lot like our North American kind, though with its longer, fancier spines and quills it is perhaps more handsome. It is no good at climbing trees but digs burrows in the ground to live in. It is found in Asia too, and in Africa. Here it truly shows the wonders of its chisel-teeth, for it can cut the hard

EUROPEAN
PORCUPINE
and
HEDGEHOG

TUFT-TAILED
PORCUPINE

Africa

teeth of other animals. It actually gnaws on the tusks of elephants which die in the jungle. Also in Africa and the East Indies is a kind which has on the end of its tail a tuft or cluster of very coarse, hollow quills, open at their ends, which it rattles when disturbed. But no porcupine of whatever kind is related to European hedgehogs, prickly though they be. Hedgehogs are not chisel-tooth rodents but insectivores. Insectivores are small animals which eat insect meat and do not gnaw. As we have seen, nature

186

uses the same scheme to protect a variety of animals and plants. Cactus is spiny. Thistles, roses, and many trees and bushes have their thorns. There are spiny mice. In the sea are the spiny sea-urchins and even porcupine fishes which can swell up and raise terrible spines on their backs when frightened. But no one of them is imitating any other. Various very different animals are protected in a similar way because a covering of spines is one of nature's schemes which happens to work for the most part very well.

12

HARES AND RABBITS

WHAT is a hare and which is a rabbit? The early settlers in America did not know. They called hares rabbits and rabbits hares, and never bothered about the differences. But there are some. Hares are born with fur and open eyes, while rabbits are born naked and blind. As a rule hares are longer-legged (especially behind) and longer-eared than rabbits. As a rule hares don't dig burrows and rabbits do. But as with every rule, there are exceptions. Our wild cottontails which live in every part of the country, our only real rabbits, mix the rules all up. Molly Cottontail seems to think she is a hare half of the time.

For instance, though her legs are short like the legs of Old World, burrow-digging rabbits, Molly seldom digs. Old World rabbits make many complicated tunnels in the ground, a great many living together. But in winter Molly prefers to live alone or with but few companions in a borrowed burrow, an empty woodchuck hole, a hollow log, any ready-made hole. But she imitates the hares completely in the summertime and has no burrow home at all. Like the hares she makes use of a form, which is the name of a favorite spot she tramples down amongst tall grass under a protecting bush or bramble. It is called a form because it fits her, being just big enough to allow turning around in comfort. Here, like a hare, she rests safely hidden during most of the day. And here in this harelike home her quartet or so of blind, naked rabbit babies are born. Just before this happens, as though she realizes that the form is not too cozy a place, she lines it with soft fur plucked from her abdomen. This also "opens her dress" and makes nursing easier. Baby hares born in similar forms are covered with wool, their eyes are open, and in a very few days they can scamper about. It is a much longer time before the helpless little cottontails can do so.

Molly's cotton tail, with its white underside, is supposed to be a safety signal for her youngsters after they begin to run about. In danger they are thought to run after the white spot into hiding. Mother carries a flag for them to follow. But this may not be so. For the babies memorize the pathways through the underbrush. Each day they run back and forth over them, a little further every day. And instead of all trying to rush after mamma, they are more likely to scatter and freeze. Even though the babies may not follow it, perhaps enemies are persuaded to. For a mother cottontail will try to lead a hunting animal away from her nest of young ones, first loudly thumping the ground to warn them of danger. But as to any other possible use for Molly's "powder puff," your own guess is as good as anyone's.

Though not as fast runners as hares, cottontails are very good dodgers and most dogs never catch them. Dogs help the hunters by routing rabbits out for a shot. But even rabbit hounds, especially raised to chase them, rarely catch one. For one thing, some dogs are such nose-minded animals they forget to use their eyes. Over and over, in winter when there were no leaves in the brush to screen his view, I have seen a rabbit hound sniffing the trail of a rabbit which was only a dozen hops away. If he had raised his head he'd have seen old bunny. But he didn't and the cottontail counted on that. She had left a trail of crisscross tracks, a crossword puzzle for the hound to wrinkle his forehead over while she quietly slipped away not the least bit worried.

When pursued by a swift dog who uses his eyes as well as his nose, or a wolf or fox, a cottontail will swim if she has to. In fact, certain kinds of cottontails swim a great deal.

BUNNY COTTONTAIL AND THE BEAGLE

MARSH RABBITS

They live mostly in the swamplands of Dixie, and are called marsh rabbits and swamp rabbits as well as just cottontails. But the cotton of their tails is dingy and not as white as the real cotton which grows on southern farms. In Georgia the marsh rabbits are called pontoons, no doubt because of their water-going habits. They swim almost as easily and nearly as much as muskrats, not only when seeking safety but just for fun. They have relatives in Central and South America.

Like most rodents which have many young ones and live on vegetables, cottontails and other hares and rabbits sometimes become a pest to farmers who kill the rodents' enemies and at the same time plant great fields of the very foods the rodents like the best. In the eastern half of our country the hunters, plus whatever hawks, foxes, weasels, etc., are still about, keep the rabbits down to reasonable numbers. They do get into gardens, and sometimes help the meadow mice gnaw bark from orchard trees, but they do not destroy everything a farmer raises the way they sometimes do in the West. There hundreds of people spread out over many miles of country and drive thousands of rabbits into corrals to be killed. Or else they lose whole haystacks and many square miles of standing grain.

In Australia, where a few pairs of European rabbits were turned loose years ago, they have even worse trouble with them. For in Australia there are no natural enemies of the rabbit unless we count a few wild dingo dogs. The Australians have great rabbit "drives" and they can tons of rabbit meat and sell millions of rabbit skins every year. But still there are always too many living and raising many families. In our own country nature kills many with disease when they become too numerous. It happens about every seven years. At that time one must be careful in buying rabbit meat, for people can become very ill with rabbit fever.

In the western mountains live the oddest hares of all. They are called haymakers from their habit of drying and storing grass and other plants for winter use. Their other names are rock rabbits, from their preference for loose rock piles as safe places to live, conys (they are not conies), little chief hares, or pikas. The pikas are about the size of guinea pigs, with no visible tail, short legs, and broad, round ears. They are the other grand rule-breakers of the hare-rabbit family. Not only are their bodies unharelike but so are their habits. No hare or rabbit except the pikas ever stores up food for winter. But in the fall these shy little mountain dwellers cut down much grass and carry it under slabs of rock. Just as there are other hares and rabbits in the Old World, so also there are pikas in Siberia. Here they are sometimes robbed by horsemen who take the pika hay to feed their horses when traveling through wild country.

Another habit which is outside the rules is bleating. Hares and rabbits seldom utter a sound except when very

badly frightened or wounded. But pikas bleat. Bleating does not quite describe the sound. No two people agree on how it should be described. One says it is a sort of squeaking bleat. Another thinks it is like the barking of a toy dog. Others hear the pika call as sharp and metallic, still another as a loud piping chirp. But all agree on one thing: the sound is very hard to locate. The pikas seem to be ventriloquists. This is easy to understand for they are colored so like the rocks that they are very hard to see. And often they call from under the rocks so that no wonder it is hard to tell just where the sound is coming from.

Also in the West, but on the great plains instead of in the mountains, live the jack rabbits, or jackass rabbits, which are truly hares both in build and habits. They have no burrows but spend the hot day in the shadow of some bit of brush or a large cactus. They depend for safety on their long ears for hearing enemies even far away, and their long legs for carrying them still farther away with amazing speed. Only greyhounds have half a chance of overtaking them. Jack rabbits have keen eyes too and as they bound away, twenty feet to a bound, they leap high in the air every so often to look back and see how the enemy is coming along.

Antelope and Black-tailed JACK RABBITS

The largest are the antelope or white-sided jack rabbits of Mexico, a few of which live in New Mexico and Arizona. Then there are the gray-sided jacks and the black-tailed jack rabbits. These are very common and may be seen at almost any time by travelers crossing the plains in automobiles or railroad trains. Tending to live further north than these are the white-tailed jacks, whose tails are entirely white, and who turn white all over every winter except for the black tips of their ears. And this brings us to their close relatives, the varying hares, the so-called snowshoe rabbits.

Varying hares change color every spring and autumn. Each fall their common dusky brown molts out while fresh white hair comes in and turns them snowy. Each spring the white hairs molt away giving place to the new brown summer suit. This varying helps a great deal since it makes these hares much harder to see than hares with unchangeable coats, at least in winter. But during spring molting when snows are melting, this scheme of nature's for concealment may quite break down. The hare may molt but the snow may not melt. This makes him a brown animal in a pure white setting. Or the snow melts before the hare molts and he becomes a pure white animal in a drab brown scene. The enemy can see him easily in either case. The same risks may recur in the fall change too. The weasel too turns white every winter, putting on his ermine overcoat not for protection but for easier hunting. But when molting and melting don't keep in step, he is the most easily spied of enemies. The hawk eats the hare and the weasel goes hungry till he catches up with winter or the first snowstorm catches up with him.

Varying hares are often called snowshoe rabbits because while the winter coats are coming in they also grow heavy pads of fur on their big hind feet and between their toes. These enable them to run over deep soft snow without the least trouble, a fine thing for safety's sake. These hares live in the mountains of our northern states and all over Canada, up to the farthest places where northern trees can grow. Here another bigger kind of white hare lives. They weigh about ten pounds and are found in all the north pole lands of both the Old World and the New. They likewise turn to a dull gray brown during the arctic summer. And of course their feet are likewise shod for snow traveling in winter. But the arctic hares have extra large and heavy claws with which to dig down through the top of the frozen world to find the moss and little scraggly plants on which they live. Even their chisel-teeth are longer and set at a sharper angle to help them get at their ice-locked landscape pantry.

In that landscape many other animals are wearing white. The arctic grouse or ptarmigan has white feathers during all the coldest part of the year. Over all the land swoop great snowy owls and gerfalcons. Where the frozen sea begins are the polar bears. Behind any rounded hummock may lurk a pure white arctic fox or an ermine-wearing weasel. They hunt the arctic hares. Great white wolves contrive to catch the hares as well. For though well equipped to run, the hares don't always start in time. Then they must serve the purpose they seem to share with other rodents in nature's plan, to act as food for animals which live on meat.

There are hares in Europe and Asia and Africa. But Europe is the place where the real rabbits first began, rabbits with the somewhat shorter legs and ears, the blind and coatless babies, and the burrows. Wild ones have always had the common gray-brown color. But since very long ago rabbits have been kept as pets by man. The Romans, on reaching the island now called England almost two thousand years ago, found the ancient Britons raising pet rabbits. Since then many special kinds have been developed. Now there are brown, black, gray, white, and mixed colored rabbits, breeds with very long hair and others with lop ears.

Rabbits have been bred very large and heavy for the meat and fur markets too. The fur is treated and made into imitations of many other animals' fur. It is used to line coats and boys' winter gloves, and the hair is used in making felt for hats and other articles. Scraps of skin from the furrier's cuttings are sold to the glue factories. And rabbit meat, especially that of rabbits raised in hutches which have not run wild and gotten tough, is very good. There are many books on rabbit raising and cookbooks give good recipes for using rabbit meat. Our government in Washington prints pamphlets on these subjects also. They tell you everything you need to know about raising rabbits, including how to raise them off the ground, which is certainly not by the ears. And none of them tell you that a rabbit's left hind foot will bring good luck, nor that Easter rabbits hatch from eggs any more than porcupines do.

It is late of a midsummer afternoon in the Catskills as the last paragraph of this book is being written. All across in the valley pastures meadow mice are enjoying ripe grass seeds. Deer mice are beginning to waken for their scampers in the attic of my house. A woodchuck has started a burrow on the hill where he means to live until next spring. Down in the stream muskrats cut water plants and swim them home like beavers. For the hundredth time, with wiggly nose, a cottontail creeps from the brush along the fence hoping for a possible hole into the garden. A red squirrel has run into the hemlocks with an astrakhan apple he cut from the tree. And surely deep in the forest some fat porcupine, comfortably seated, reaches out hooked claws and pulls sweet birch twigs to him.

I have always liked the creatures who belong to the chisel-tooth tribe. But now that I have written a book about them I really think I like them even better. And now that you have read it, let us hope you like them even better too.

CPSIA information can be obtained at www.ICGtesting.com
Printed in the USA
LVOW12s0011050515

437173LV00004B/251/P